Annika
and the
Treasure of Iceland

By Antje Bothin

BeulAithris

Publishing

Scotland

First published 2023

ISBN: 9798853479227

1

Gunnar Karlson's tyres incessantly rolled towards his desired destination. It was dark and the road was barely visible. He was terribly exhausted. He could hardly keep his eyes open because he had been on the move for ten hours. But he was glad that he had got a coffee and a sandwich at the petrol station. He had to stay awake at all costs now.

Gunnar continuously steered his truck straight ahead. He yawned. Despite long breaks, he really had to pay attention so that he did not fall asleep. The panting noise of the engine additionally seemed tiring. He struggled to focus his eyes on the road. Would he get there in time?

It was secluded in Iceland and sometimes the roads could already get slippery in autumn. There was no snow there yet, but it was cold. The heating of his truck had to work hard. The air around him smelled of diesel. He had opened the window a tiny crack to let fresh air in.

The car radio played soft rock music. Gunnar sang along quietly and while doing so he tapped his finger rhythmically on the wheel. Instantly, he felt more alert. Was he speeding? - he pondered for a second, worried the sentimental song could have distracted him. Suddenly, there was a greenish light in the sky. He could see it well, it was beautiful. But as he looked up, he reckoned his truck had skidded briefly. The northern lights were a mysterious natural spectacle but not unusual in these latitudes. Surely they would accompany him through this long night.

But then he saw a glaring light in a different colour, man-made and as blue as the ice-cold water of the Atlantic. It was flashing wildly in the grey landscape directly in front of him. Gunnar instinctively sensed danger. Then he recognised a police officer in a black uniform standing in the light cone of his headlights.

2

Annika Magnusdottir was restless that night. She tossed and turned in her bed, from left to right and seconds later to the left again and so on. Without stopping. She could not suppress these thoughts. What if something bad happened? There were so many what ifs. In a doze, she heard a noise that came from outside. It sounded like wild animals.

'They can't sleep either,' she thought.

The day before, something quite strange had happened to her. She had received a mysterious message containing an invitation:

'Would you like to take part in a Treasure Hunt if so come to Hotel Islandia, Reykjavik, 11 am!'

At first, Annika was scared to participate. But her mother was planning a birthday party with family friends and Annika did not want to attend. People would say that she was very quiet, and Annika hated such comments. The guests came from further away and were likely to stay for longer. So having a reason for not being home would come in handy. And her mother usually encouraged her to leave the house more often. This was her chance to try and do so. She was eager to go there. It sounded luxurious and food and drink were available for free. And Reykjavik was interesting, as it is the capital of Iceland. She just hoped that she would not need to talk much there.

The bed was nicely warm at least and she held her cuddly toy tightly in her hand. Max was cute like all cuddly toys but also robust. She had always loved Max much since she was little. Perhaps too much. The scuffed spots in his fur were proof of that. His loyal eyes always looked at her. He had cute ears and a snub nose.

Her mother had bought her a new teddy long ago, but Annika loved her Max. He had protected her as a child and as she had slowly become an adult. Max was always there.

'I need to fall asleep now,' Annika heard her inner voice say.

But the more she tried, the less it worked. Perhaps she should get up for a while and wait until she was really tired? She stayed in bed even though she knew better. It was just too unpleasant to leave her bed because not all rooms in the house were heated at night.

Time passed.

Eventually, it was time to get up and Annika was sure she had not slept all night. She was so excited because of the treasure hunt that would start today.

Annika was 21 years old and did not talk much. Due to her muteness with strangers, she got into trouble a lot. She should have been taken to a doctor as a young child and received a diagnosis. Two complicated words.

Selective mutism.

Annika would not have understood these words as a child.

But now it was just a label. It said so in a book she had read. Perhaps situational mutism or even situational speaking would be a better name because the word selective sounds like a choice, but it actually means specific in the world of science. And selective mutism is not a choice!

She had probably been suffering from this since early childhood. It had made it impossible for her to speak freely in certain situations. Especially when other people were within earshot. But in other situations, she could talk normally. She was very sure of this now. Because she had these memories.

When she started nursery, she simply remained mute. All day long, she did not speak a single word, she did not laugh, she did not cry. Once she fell from the swing in the morning while playing at the nursery, but nobody had noticed it. Her knee was bleeding and internally she screamed in pain, but she did not let it show. She did not make a face. Nobody came to know it. It was not till her mother picked her up in the evening that the wound was noticed. Her mother was shocked but that was normal for Annika.

Annika was very talkative at home and even cheeky, but she was very quiet with strangers. That was not a choice. She simply could not talk then. The words got stuck in her mind.

It was as if there were two Annikas, the loud, lively girl at home and the silent shadow of herself in public. It was unbearable to be called names and thought of as unkind when she did not manage to say hello or thank you to people.

Most people had never heard of her problem and expected so much. Annika had only known for a short time that her silence had a name. A diagnosis.

Selective mutism.

As a child, she had believed she was just too stupid to talk. And she was the only person in the world that had such a problem. She was desperate and was bullied a lot. Her classmates said she was stuck-up. Often, she simply got overlooked, forgotten or excluded. Her parents and teachers had her down as shy or stubborn. That is why she had not received any help as a child.

'She'll grow out of it when she gets older,' they had always said.

Annika was an adult now and knew better. She had not got rid of these stupid speech blocks. Not yet. But she desperately wanted to do something about it.

Annika had no friends and spent most of her time alone at home. She had successfully finished school somehow despite occasional bad oral marks, but she had not gained ground on the job market as yet.

She wanted to study but it was not that easy because talking was required everywhere. And she did not know what she would like to study. There were so many fields of study, and everything appeared to be so complicated to her. Not because of the theoretical subject matter but because of the social side. Would she get along with all these people on the campus? Could she give talks and collaborate with others on hands-on projects? Possibly discuss problems in groups? Where would she live? And where would the money to live on come from when everything was constantly getting more expensive? So many frightening questions. She felt absolutely not ready for these and unable to cope.

She would not have dreamed that one day she would take part in this crazy race.

A treasure hunt all around Iceland.

3

Such a major event had not taken place here before. It was the first one of its kind in the world, ever. The excitement among the participants was huge. Most of them had not been able to think of anything else for some time. They had all been invited to this place like Annika and asked themselves what would be in store for them now.

There was a sad reason for this. A famous rich man recently died. Fridrik Jonsson had been 99 years old, and he had left behind a strange wish. There was supposed to be a treasure hidden somewhere on the island. That is what it said in his will. It was hidden somewhere on the island. Nobody knew where. But the old man's last will contained detailed instructions for an adventurous treasure hunt. The alleged treasure promised its lucky finder extraordinary fame and massive wealth. Rumour had it there were precious pieces of jewellery made of pure gold.

Professor Inga Hansdottir had the honourable task of leading the treasure hunt. This is how the deceased had ordered it. The Professor was 59 years old and lived on her own in a much too big house since her children had moved out. Their rooms had been empty for a long time and the furniture had slowly begun to get dusty. All toys were packed away in boxes waiting to be rediscovered by her grandchildren.

The silence in the house was unbearable. Inga liked to remind herself of her children's laughter from times gone by. Despite her slogan 'knowledge is power', the academic loved to knit. She did so every evening, in front of the television with a glass of wine. She preferred a simple pattern that repeated itself. She had already knitted countless hats but at the moment, she was working on a blue scarf. While she was knitting, she felt the soft wool between her fingers, which she found very relaxing.

Inga was an educated woman, and she could organise things. That was important for such a treasure hunt. She gave lectures at university that needed to be well planned. She had published research that was internationally renowned. She was distinguished in her field and loved her work. Nevertheless, she looked forward to her retirement.

Inga had chosen the treasure hunt participants according to the wishes of the old man. How exactly remained her secret. Perhaps they were all listed in the telephone book, and she had worked it out scientifically. Perhaps it was random. But they had all come to her at Reykjavik in order to find this treasure.

'Welcome everyone!' Inga said and looked at the crowd of prospective treasure hunters. Her voice sounded pleasant. She wore a light blue blouse and dark blue trousers.

Nine excited people were now here in front of her and they were waiting curiously for the beginning of the adventure. They were sitting on hard chairs in a semi-circle. There were full water bottles on the tables. Still water and carbonated water was available. There was fresh fruit in baskets on the tables. Grapes, apples and bananas. Some participants had already helped themselves. They made an effort to listen to Inga's remarks. Gunnar and Annika were among them. Gunnar was in a good mood because the police officers that he had seen at the roadside in the night had not wanted anything from him. They had been busy with broken-down vehicles.

Gunnar had been a truck driver for a long time, and he always wanted to experience something new. He was fascinated by the idea of a treasure hunt, as he knew the roads of Iceland very well. He had fewer and fewer assignments lately and now he had his truck at his disposal. Somehow the vehicle was his home. Gunnar loved his music and his old maps. They would get him to his destination without any problems. Surely he would find this treasure very quickly and forget his worries while doing so.

Since his wife had left him, he had not been in this area. Their divorce was planned, and all the red tape related to that. He had loved her and still did. But she had gone to America with his best friend. For a better life, she had said. What did either of them know about America?

Gunnar had been to America. He found it interesting but somehow too much of everything. Everything was huge. Oversized. Houses too big, roads too big, too many people. Contrary to Gunnar's relatively slender physique, most people in America were obese. They must have fed on unhealthy things, he had thought. Burger and pizza instead of fruit and vegetables. Had his doctor not advised him to eat a balanced diet and to exercise more, now that he was getting older? He also needed to drink less coffee and stop smoking.

That was his intention. He had thrown away his last cigarettes weeks ago and now he tried to get along without them. This distraction had come to him at the right time, as he often realised that he longed for his old habits. But he simply had to have at least one cup of coffee a day. At 45 years of age, he slowly had to start paying attention to his health or he would not be able to experience his retirement. His blond hair and blue eyes did not stand out much among the people in the town. His clothing, a black t-shirt, dark jeans and a green jacket, also was unobtrusive.

Annika dreamed of freedom. She had dressed herself especially smartly for this event. She wore a warm jacket and dark trousers. Naturally, she had sat down away from everyone and on her own, her back facing the wall. Her bag was under the table. She did not want to draw attention to herself. She was very quiet. When she received the invitation for the treasure hunt, she saw that as a sign that she had to become more confident. She needed a meaningful task. She was ready for an adventure. But she did not know yet that she would have to leave Reykjavik to explore the most remote corners of Iceland.

Annika stared at the young man to the left of her. Somehow she felt attracted to him. He was really handsome. She did not have any experience with the opposite sex yet. But she needed to pay attention and listen now. What she did not know was that the man's name was Ragnar Lokisson. And Ragnar was looking for happiness. He wanted to see the world. The treasure hunt promised to be an unforgettable experience that was why he could not decline this invitation. The dance instructor was thrilled to be here. His favourite drink was water and he had already helped himself. His golden-yellow hat concealed his hair. His eyes looked in the direction of Inga. He did not seem to notice Annika.

Inga had been sitting with everyone in the meeting room of this modern hotel for a while. She noticed that this girl, Annika, was exceptionally quiet but did not say anything. Inga explained again to all participants in detail what this treasure hunt was about. She then took a piece of paper that was on the table in front of her. There was not much on it. Only a few lines.

Inga read the poem aloud. It was a riddle.

> *In this corner starts great fortune*
> *Examine the connection, do it soon*
> *Where Europe and America meet*
> *Your dreams came true greet!*

'What's that supposed to mean?' someone shouted in bewilderment.

The rich old man had apparently been a joker. Annika and Ragnar looked at each other in silence. Gunnar's eyes twinkled. He seemed to know what these lines meant. The other participants also seemed to have understood the poem. A man and a woman were standing in a corner next to the exit.

'Let's go!' she said.

The man grabbed his coat and put it on slowly.

Inga put the piece of paper back on the table and looked out of the window. It was raining. The room was relatively dark, only the soft light of the ceiling lamp was shining down on her. She felt a touch of cold scamper down her back and suddenly she craved for a hot bath.

'Not now,' she thought.

Business before pleasure. She looked around the room sheepishly and saw the woman and the man. A smile ran across her face. Then she remembered something very important.

'And I also have to mention, should anyone think about cheating, unfortunately, they'll automatically be disqualified if this can be proven! The treasure must fall into decent hands. Let's agree for the sake of fairness, right?'

A murmur went through the crowd but most of the prospective treasure hunters nodded. Stress showed on their faces. At the end, Inga wished all participants good luck and sent them out into the world on a treasure hunt.

The race had begun.

4

Anton Olafson went straight to the hotel bar after the disclosure of the riddle. He needed a whiskey now. And he had to think. Did the old joker mean a meeting between European and American politicians? Was there one recently in Reykjavik? He could not remember anything. He scratched his head. Who was he anyway? And what did he know about politics? The drink tasted good. He was used to quite a lot and he did not get drunk immediately. He began to lose himself in his thoughts.

Anton believed that he was the best gardener in the world but the payment for his job was not so good. He dreamed of finally being free from debt. The gardener from Grindavik had a lot of girlfriends but he could not always give them what they dreamed of. His lifestyle exceeded his funds and he also had to repay the mortgage for his house. This treasure hunt came right on cue.

His hobby, diving, sucked up huge amounts of money. Anton loved merrymaking and adventures. He had a real good time when gambling. He did not care whether it was illegal. He just could not get caught. The world was not fair. He would do everything in his power to find this treasure first. He was not a coward! And he was on leave. Suddenly a pretty blonde caught Anton's eye and he ordered another drink. He moved closer to her and looked her in the eye.

'Hey, sweetie, fancy a trip to my bedroom?' he whispered into her ear.

The young lady appeared to be disgusted.

'Forget it!' she stood up and left.

'Well, then don't!' he thought to himself unhappily. 'The ladies aren't the way they used to be.'

He was slightly drunk, and his mind was beginning to work hard.

Was he not good enough for her? Anton took a sip and stared at the wall. He saw photos of volcanoes and snow-covered mountains. Some photos were of bathers in the sea. One picture bore the title *Westman Islands 1973*.

Was there a volcanic eruption there back then, he wondered, as what was depicted there looked like that. He looked at the rest of the wall. A map of Iceland with illustrations of famous tourist sites was also hanging there. Suddenly he knew what he was looking for.

'The bridge between the continents of Europe and America! Of course that was what the rhyme was about.'

He drank up quickly, paid and made his way outside. He now had to find a way to get to the bridge as soon as possible.

5

Margret Einarsdottir and Oskar Baldursson left the hotel building quickly. Both were elegantly dressed. Margret had been to the hairdressers to make sure her hair conveyed the right impression. She wore the latest perfume and a silver necklace with matching earrings. For Oskar, it was the black suit, as usual.

'We need to go to that bridge,' she whispered into her husband's ear. 'Do you remember? There, where we kissed for the first time.'

'That's almost ten years ago,' Oskar replied.

'How could I ever forget about that.'

Margret and Oskar were a happy couple. Their mutual dream was a good life. Both were in their mid-thirties and had steady jobs. They were not poor, but more possessions were better than fewer. They were on leave and had a lot of time for a treasure hunt. Both had got to know each other in a church in Reykjavik. Or better up on the observation tower of the church one summer's evening.

The magnificent Hallgrímskirkja stood on a hill in the town. Being the biggest church in Iceland, it towered above the neighbouring houses. A great example of architecture in the shape of a glacier that could not be overlooked. Both of them had gone up onto the roof individually and had been amazed by the view. It was warm and the sun was shining. The view was phenomenal in all directions. Margret wanted to take a photo. Oskar helped her with that. He offered to take a photo of her in front of the backdrop of the town. Margret agreed. They immediately clicked. Eventually, they arranged to meet for coffee in a cosy street cafe. And the rest is history, as the saying goes.

Margret was looking for work at the time. She was young and pretty. Oskar was an engineer. He had been enthusiastic about technical detail drawings at school and loved to occupy himself with architecture. He really enjoyed studying. In particular, Oskar liked bridges. That is why he immediately knew what Margret meant when she talked about the bridge. A week after their encounter at the church Oskar invited Margret to go on an excursion. He wanted to show her a special place. They went to the Reykjanes Peninsula and to the bridge between the continents by car. The scenery was barren, but the bridge was well visible. Oskar positioned himself at the edge.

'The European and the North American plates meet here,' he said proudly.

'Great. All the things you know!' Margret replied.

She discovered a sign with a description of the sight.

'It says here, the Eurasian plate,' she corrected him flirtatiously.

'I'm going over to America now.'

She laughed.

And she crossed the bridge.

'Sure, you geography genius,' Oskar grumbled and followed her.

They went back and forth several times and joked.

Then it happened.

Oskar pulled her close towards himself and his lips touched hers. It was a passionate kiss.

Both of them were very close and were soon one heart and one soul.

Shortly after, both were happily married.

Later, Margret got a job as a secretary with Oskar's company. Since then she had been working there. That was good. But she longed for more freedom.

6

The taxi driver Jonas Gislason hoped to gain extra income from the treasure. The 63-year-old wanted to enjoy his retirement soon. But with his beggarly taxi driver wages, his pension would not be very high. Jonas got into his taxi after the meeting, and he was very excited. He saw his grey hair in the mirror. A deep wrinkle on his forehead was also evidence of his life experience. He could go anywhere. It did not matter, he retired soon. But he did not think of the consequences of his deeds, he only had the riddle in mind. He brooded loudly.

A corner? Well, there is the Peninsula in the southwest where the airport is. And a connection? Where Europe and America meet?

He thought a while.

'I know,' he exclaimed suddenly.

He took his navigation device and set it to look for a route to the bridge on the Peninsula. While his taxi swept through the streets of Reykjavik, he remembered a special passenger. It was about two years ago, when he allowed an old man to get into his vehicle at a street corner. He had wanted to go to the airport. The traffic was abysmal, and the weather was bad. They stood car-to-car on the main road in a traffic jam, his car was only slowly moving forward. The rain crackled against the windowpane.

'Drive faster!' the man had demanded forcefully. 'I'll miss my plane!'

'Where are you going?'

'To London.'

The old man leaned back. 'I really don't want to be late.'

'We'll get there!' Jonas exclaimed. 'Just let me do it.'

It seemed as if all traffic lights now started to switch to green as they approached. And then the traffic and the weather got quickly better when they left the capital. The taxi driver arrived at the airport in time for the flight.

'Thank you very much,' the passenger said to Jonas and gave him a generous tip.

After that, Jonas had gone home immediately so that he did not miss the football match on television - he had loved football since his childhood. Jonas rubbed his forehead. He remembered that day so clearly. That must have been Fridrik Jonsson, the creator of this treasure hunt.

7

Ragnar was dancing. That is what he did most of the time. And his golden hat was dancing with him. He had plugged his earphones into his ears and was loudly singing along to his favourite song. He had got up in a good mood today and he was still in high spirits, as the treasure hunt had finally started. Ragnar was really looking forward to this new challenge and the adventure that was waiting for him.

Yesterday, he had been in his dance studio and had shown his students a few new steps. Teaching dance, he worked with adults and children. Ragnar could glide across the dance floor like a swan and forget everything. Any worries disappeared from his mind as soon as he entered the dance floor.

Discofox was on the agenda yesterday. He had kept his legs moving elegantly and full of verve. The rhythm of the music stirred up emotions. The light in the ballroom was bright. The air smelled of sweet flowers. That was surely thanks to Rita, Mona and Karina. His students used deodorant and perfume liberally. When they were dancing, they often said Ragnar was the best dance instructor in the world. Ragnar sometimes blushed a little then. Nevertheless, he liked such compliments. But now, his staff members had to get along without him, now that he was not there. He had to find the treasure.

Ragnar swept away the memory and slowly walked along the hotel corridor. Annika was close by. He smiled at her. His grey eyes were fixated on the exit. His sporty trousers covered his thin legs and his colourful shirt looked good on him. They both used the lift to go down then and a little later the two were standing in front of the door of the hotel. They probably both knew what to do but Annika had a giant problem.

8

Sigrun Halldorsdottir and Helga Ingolfsdottir had left the hotel like everyone else. They had each got into their cars and had made their way to this bridge. For both, this destination had spontaneously come to mind as the riddle's solution because they knew this end to the south of Reykjavik pretty well.

Helga wanted to have it nice at home. She lived in a village and coddled her grandchildren. She bought them countless toys. Conservative like she was, the little girl got a doll and later new clothes for the doll. And she gave toy cars and trains to the little boy. Of course, there were always new models. Perhaps the good-natured granny was a little naive. Her glasses almost slid from her nose. But a treasure hunt also aroused her interest. She was not too old yet for a little bit of fun!

Sigrun was convinced that the treasure would soon be hers. The attractive actress wore a fashionable suit and could perform any role. She wanted to prove that women would be able to take part in a treasure hunt. She had time at the moment, as she had a shooting break. Her new film in America was planned for next year, the date was already certain. Sigrun had hardly left Reykjavik when she realised she needed to refuel. She had forgotten that this morning, she thought angrily.

She drove to a petrol station at the roadside and found a free petrol pump, opened the lid of the tank, put the pump into the tank and afterwards out of the tank again and went to the small shop and paid. Sigrun was lucky, as there was nobody in front of her and everything was very fast. Then she got back into her car again and opened the glove compartment. She had had a travel guidebook in the glove compartment for years and she dug it out from between old maps. It was a booklet with the majestic Hallgrímskirkja on the front cover, it almost looked like new. She looked up the entry about the bridge and read:

'*The bridge leads over a crack in a lava field. It is a symbol for the connection of the continental plates and has become an important tourist attraction.*'
Sigrun closed the travel guide again.

She had bought it because she intended to visit Iceland's sights one day. Unfortunately, she had never had the chance and she forgot about the book. This treasure hunt had given her the unexpected opportunity to put her plan from the past into practice. Where else would the adventure take her?

9

Annika had immediately gone outside after the meeting. She had to reach the bridge very quickly. She had read about it in a book recently. What connection in a corner would the riddle mean otherwise? But how would she get there, she asked herself unhappily.

She did not have a car or a driving licence. She did not know whether there was a bus going in that direction at all, or whether it would still go there at this time. But she did not believe it. A short glance at the sign at the bus stop in front of the hotel confirmed it. She had to find another way. She was desperate.

During the announcement of the riddle, a man had already attracted her attention. He was handsome and they stared at each other all the time. She had wanted to say something simple like 'Hello' but that was endlessly difficult. She had clearly seen in his eyes that he also seemed to know where this treasure hunt would lead them. The man made a good impression and she wanted to try it. Now she was standing nervously next to this man whose name she did not know. She wanted to speak to him, ask him for his name but she could not get herself to do it. There were many people in the street, and they passed them both by. Annika just thought – 'NO ONE MUST HEAR when I speak to him.'

But people were unfortunately close by all the time. She could not ask his name. It was not possible. Her tongue was heavy, and her throat was parched. She felt stiff and helpless. Her lips were glued together; her mouth was just an expressionless line.

Ragnar also seemed to find the moment strange. He had seen how she had gone to the bus stop and had followed her.

'Hello,' he said to Annika. 'Are you also on the treasure hunt?'

Annika did not reply.

She tried to nod but it was hardly visible.

'I've seen you inside. The riddle was cool, wasn't it? But it's very easy, isn't it?' He continued, 'I'm leaving right away, it's obvious where we need to go.'

No reaction from Annika. She looked down awkwardly. But that did not bother Ragnar. He was used to shy dance students and he simply continued doing what he always did in such a case. He kept on talking. His kind manner made him appear trustworthy.

'Oh, I haven't introduced myself yet. I'm Ragnar. Nice to meet you.'

Annika kept on looking at the ground and said nothing. Ragnar kept talking.

'What's wrong? Do you need help?'

'Is there no bus today?'

'Well, you don't have a car?'

'Hey, I really ask myself whether you might want to come with me?'

'I can give you a lift.'

'You'll be just standing at the bus stop forever.'

'And I'm here now.'

'I'm not going to harm you.'

'Ragnar is quite nice,' Annika thought.

'It would be nice to get to know your name.'

'If only I knew. Let me guess! Tina? Or Lisa?'

'What else could it be? You look like a Maria.'

'Perhaps you'd like to tell me later?'

'Really, it's getting cold.'

'Well, come with me!'

He went to his car and Annika followed him silently.

Ragnar's behaviour helped Annika. He did not mock her for her silence. He seemed to accept it. Why, she did not know.

People would usually be offended. They got aggressive or just went away immediately. But he was talking like a sports commentator; he simply vocalised what he saw and thought. And he appeared to be terribly kind. He did not seem to expect answers to his questions, and he obviously wanted to help her. Exactly what she wanted. But was it dangerous to go with a stranger, an unknown man? She had her doubts, but she had no choice in this case.

10

Ragnar drove a golden medium-sized vehicle that was elegant. Annika stared at the posh car, wide-eyed. She did not know much about cars but this one impressed her. He had parked in the hotel car park in the open and his car was standing in a row with the cars of the other hotel guests.

Ragnar held the key in his hand and pressed the button on the remote control. The orange car lights flashed briefly, and the doors opened. He got into the car and Annika sat down in the front passenger seat.

Now they were alone. Annika tried to say something again. But Ragnar beat her to it. He continued talking.

'You like music, don't you?'

'I'll turn on the radio.'

'But I'm still interested in your name.'

Ragnar pressed a button on the car radio and smiled at her. As there was no reply, he drove off.

'Annika,' Annika said softly after a few seconds.

Too softly.

The driving noises and the radio were too loud. Ragnar had not heard her.

'What did you say? Sorry, I was distracted.'

'Annika... my name is Annika,' she repeated.

'Oh, nice. That's a lovely name.'

'Relax. We're going to this corner.'

'You know where, don't you? To the bridge between the continents.'

The vehicle went along the streets taking them closer to their destination. They left Reykjavik and arrived at the highway and on the Reykjanes Peninsula. The area got more and more remote, and the roads became smaller and smaller and emptier.

'We almost need to go to the end,' Ragnar said.

The weather had deteriorated. Suddenly, it was raining and storming. Ragnar drove very slowly because he could hardly see anything.

'By the way, I'm a dance instructor,' he said to Annika.

Annika looked at the road ahead. She suddenly cringed but she said nothing. There was something on the road. She saw a dark shadow. Ragnar did not seem to notice. He kept on talking happily.

'Dancing means freedom. It's relaxing and...'

'Ah!'

'Oh, no!'

Ragnar had slammed on the brakes. His vehicle had come to a halt about half a metre in front of the obstacle. The bright light from the headlights showed what was lying there.

It was a giant pile of debris. Bricks and broken paint cans had dyed the road surface in all colours. Shattered wooden poles stuck out in all directions. They looked like monsters out of an old film. A truck had obviously dropped some of its load. The building materials blocked the way.

'Phew, that just went well,' Ragnar groaned. 'Are you ok?'

Annika nodded. She was shaking all over.

'Are you sure? You're so pale.'

'Yes. It's only the shock,' Annika uttered.

She opened the window a little bit. Somehow she felt sick. She took a deep breath and felt that it got better. Don't pass out she willed herself.

'If we'd got these on the head...,' Ragnar pondered.

'I don't want to think about that.'

'We were really lucky.'

A long pause followed. Both kept silent. Ragnar slowly calmed down and began to think clearly again.

A gnawing thought suddenly hit him.

'Oh dear, how are we going to get on now?'

11

Fridrik Jonsson had left another riddle at the bridge between the continents. The treasure hunters just had to find it and understand what they had to do next. The buried treasure was obviously somewhere out there.

Annika and Ragnar were lucky because they were not delayed for long. The obstacle had already been reported to the police and they realised that when they suddenly heard loud noises. Helpers removed everything quickly and they were able to continue their journey unscathed.

Meanwhile, Gunnar and Anton arrived at the bridge at about the same time. They had not been delayed. Gunnar had parked his truck on the main road and had walked to the bridge. He stepped on the bridge, looked down and saw Anton down below; he was poking the ground with a stick.

'What is he doing down there,' Gunnar asked himself.

He had recognised Anton immediately - he had seen this face before.

As nobody else was there, he shouted 'Is the treasure buried there?'

But Anton could not hear him because of the strong winds and did not respond.

At this moment, Annika and Ragnar arrived at the scene of action and they both saw Gunnar and Anton.

'Don't let us be too late,' Ragnar thought.

'Hello colleague,' he said to Gunnar.

'Did you find anything?'

'Unfortunately not. But maybe he did down there.'

'Oh!'

Ragnar wanted to take a closer look.

Meanwhile, Annika was standing quietly next to Gunnar and stared at Anton full of expectation. Her jacket was completely puffed up because of the strong winds and the ends of her scarf were wildly flying around in the air. She felt uncomfortable being here, but not just because of the weather.

Ragnar was also down there now. He looked around without saying a word. Then he walked across to Anton.

'So, you found anything?'

Anton just grumbled something unintelligible.

'Pardon?'

'Nope. I'm just looking, it could be anywhere here.'

'Yes, of course. I'm going to the other side,' Ragnar said.

He went under the bridge and suddenly stopped.

'Everyone, come here!' he all of a sudden shouted excitedly.

Anton, Gunnar and Annika ran as fast as they could under the bridge. And then they saw it all.

So it was under the bridge, on a stone. The next riddle. A new clue and unfortunately no treasure. Somebody had sprayed the text on the wall in a bright red colour, easy to read.

Further into the mainland, go
Where Strokkur provides a show
Come to the Great Geysir
The path to joy is here!

The remaining participants arrived shortly after and also found and solved the riddle. Jonas had chosen the way through the valley first and had stopped short under the bridge. Helga and Sigrun had met Margret and Oskar on the road, and they had then discovered the poem together. Everyone was on their way to the next destination and a little bit closer to the treasure.

12

The road led all treasure hunters back the way they had come across the long Reykjanes Peninsula, past Reykjavik, and then inland. This route was generally known as a part of the Golden Circle. It offered many sights, and they were not too far away from the capital.

Ragnar had turned on the music again.

'Great,' Annika thought.

She liked the song very much. She knew the lyrics by heart. She wanted to sing along but Ragnar's presence did not allow that.

'NO ONE MUST HEAR!' she thought. How embarrassing it would be for her if Ragnar heard her sing.

She only managed to move her lips, which was barely visible, but no sound came out. But in her mind, she sang along. The journey had already taken a while and Annika slowly relaxed. 'It is just wonderful to be out and about here,' she thought.

The Icelandic countryside passed by outside the window. She felt a feeling of freedom emerge. It had been a long day and she was tired. Ragnar also looked tired.

As if it was magic, he suddenly said, 'I believe we must find a bed.'

Then he yawned loudly. Suddenly, there was a loud bang.

'What was that?' Ragnar exclaimed in surprise.

In the rear mirror, he suddenly saw another car that drove up very closely to his car.

'He hit us!'

The unknown car kept on driving way too closely. It did not make any attempts to brake. But Ragnar could not recognise the driver. Still he assumed that it was a man.

'He did that on purpose! What does he want from us?'

Annika had roused from her doze and looked over her shoulder. She now saw the car, too.

Then she nervously looked over to Ragnar and said,
'I'm scared.'

Bang.

'Ah!' Ragnar screamed. 'This can't be happening!'

The car had hit them on purpose. It was the second time.
Ragnar slowed down, he wanted to give way. The car changed
lane at lightning speed and overtook them. It was so fast that it
was out of view within seconds. Ragnar was angry and could
not believe what had just happened.

'I must be dreaming. That's only possible in action films.'

Unfortunately, he had not seen the number plate. It was just
a car, like the thousands of them on the roads of Iceland. A
make unknown to him and an unremarkable featureless colour.

'Everything ok?' he whispered to Annika.

She nodded.

Ragnar looked for a suitable place to stop and got out of his
car. He examined the damage closely. Luckily, it was only a
small dent under the boot. The golden colour was partially
splintered but it was hardly visible.

'Darn,' he fumed. 'My beautiful car!' Then he got back in.

'Is it bad?' Annika asked tentatively.

'It won't stop us, but my car has just dropped in value,' he
replied sarcastically and also a little sadly.

'I'm sorry.'

Annika suddenly got frightened of herself. She had just
talked so much with Ragnar. But the two of them were alone in
the car and nobody else was listening. That is why she could
do it. She knew that from now on it would be possible with
Ragnar. The ice was broken. But the adventure had left its
mark and she was overwhelmed by stress and exhaustion. The
anxiety was deep down inside her, but it was not visible.

'So what. Let's keep going,' Ragnar said and then he started
the engine and drove off.

13

Ragnar and Annika spent the night in the car covered in warm blankets. Due to exhaustion, they had not even looked for vacant rooms at all. Annika had pulled her hat and scarf over her face. That way, the cold was reasonably bearable.

'If only Max was here,' she thought. But unfortunately the cuddly toy was sitting at home on her warm and soft bed.

Annika closed her eyes. She was fast asleep.

And then she woke up again.

It had only been a few hours of sleep. She was too excited to sleep for long and did so only because she was tired. When Annika woke up, she messaged her mother to let her know that she was fine. And if she needed anything, she would buy it. But Ragnar had rested well and was able to drive on now that the new day had begun. The music playing in the car radio perked him up.

As they went deeper inland, the road got narrower. They found a place to stop. Ragnar turned the radio off so that they could speak with each other more easily.

'Here you are, Annika, please take a look at the map,' Ragnar said and handed an atlas of Iceland to her.

'I reckon we took a wrong turn earlier.'

'I'm still completely stiff from sleeping. The seat wasn't really comfortable.'

Ragnar had a stretch and took a sip of his water bottle. With relish, he then took a bite of his sandwich. Fortunately, he had remembered to bring along provisions.

Annika had already eaten a banana and now she was looking for the spot on the map where they actually were.

'Where are we?'

'I can't find it. Is there a signpost anywhere here?' she asked.

She was becoming more familiar with Ragnar and could talk better and better to him. Almost normally. Like at home, loudly and spontaneously. Whatever had to be said, what she thought and what she wanted to say.

'I'll get out and take a look,' Ragnar replied.

Annika rummaged and looked at the list of places. She hummed to herself.

'La la la la la.'

The song that had been playing on the radio yesterday was stuck in her head. It was a catchy tune. But that did not matter because it made Annika cheerful. Then she remembered and kept a lookout for Ragnar. He was nowhere to be seen. 'Where did he go?' she wondered. She kept on singing and smiled. Then she turned on the radio again. The news was on. She turned it off again very quickly.

'Oh, no feel-good music,' she muttered to herself. Annika did not like spoken utterances on the radio.

And she particularly did not like news broadcasts. All the evil of the world gave her a terrible fright. For this reason, the radio and television set often had to be turned off at home when natural disasters, bad accidents and suchlike were on. Or they changed channels quickly.

Ragnar was still not back. Annika slowly got anxious. She was all alone in this area and did not even know where exactly she was. She did have her phone with her, but it was questionable whether that would help her much, as the battery was almost flat and there was no signal. Unfortunately, this happened often in this lonely wilderness off the main road. Many people did not live here, nature ruled. 'Singing helps, when I'm scared,' she thought and came back to the song.

Eventually, she saw Ragnar turn around the corner.

'Phew!'

He was not lost. He got into the car again and took the atlas. Then he showed Annika a road with his finger.

'We must be here. Do you see? At least, that's what I think. And there is where we want to go.'

He pointed to another spot on the map.

'That's not too far,' Annika said.

'Okay, let's go then,' Ragnar replied.

'And you tell me where we need to go please.'

'Aye, aye, Sir!' Annika joked and laughed loudly.

Then she planned a suitable route to their destination. 'We have lost so much time,' she thought anxiously.

14

'I wonder if the others are already there?' Ragnar said. He was wearing his golden hat as always.

'I'm afraid so but who cares,' Annika replied.

'We'll find it, for sure,' Ragnar assured her.

They knew that they had to go to the Great Geysir and to Strokkur. These are hot springs in Iceland that are often visited by tourists. Both of them were sitting in Ragnar's car and enjoying the journey. Annika's hair smelled of flowery shampoo. She had washed her hair at home before this adventure had started. Annika loved the scent and Ragnar also seemed to like it. Annika appealed to him.

Suddenly, Ragnar looked worried.

'We need to refuel,' he said then.

Via the display on the car dashboard, he had seen that the tank was nearly empty. Annika grabbed her phone and smiled. It still had power left. And there was a signal again. It was even a strong signal because they were in an inhabited area again.

'All right, I'll find out where the next petrol station is.'

'Well, none near here.'

'Oh, I forgot to refuel in town.'

Ragnar frowned.

'What are we going to do now? We'll stop if we don't refuel immediately!' he exclaimed.

'Don't you have a fuel can?' Annika asked.

'No, I have no space for that. Besides it's dangerous.'

'You have a point there,' Annika replied. 'We'll have to take a detour again. There's one in this place here.' She handed Ragnar the atlas and showed him the place using her finger.

'So we need to go there now,' Ragnar said.

'Okay, turn right at the junction,' Annika instructed him.

They found the small place and the petrol station. Ragnar dealt with that while Annika studied the atlas more closely.

When Ragnar got in again, she said, 'We need to get going quickly!'

The landscape was dreary but interesting. There were green bushes everywhere. It was relatively flat on one side but there were mountains in sight. They reached their original road again.

Nothing could stop them now.

15

The landscape was getting a little more mountainous and it suddenly began to snow.

'Oh, nope!' Ragnar groaned. 'Now winter is on its way. I've got shovel and broom with me, but I hope the road will be clear and gritted.'

It was snowing more and more heavily. The snowflakes were dancing on the car windows. Annika found them very pretty but unfortunately also very inconvenient. They would lengthen their journey time immensely and the competition never slept. She was certain that the others had arrived ages ago, had already solved the riddle and had claimed the treasure for themselves.

These thoughts tortured Annika. She often worried about pretty much everything. That is why she had so many fears. Not only regarding talking but also concerning many other things. Water, fire, thunderstorms, dogs, spiders. Rocks that could fall off cliffs. She always saw danger. Threats were ultimately everywhere. The world was an uncertain place. Her mind wanted to ruminate and ponder way too much. And most of the time she imagined negative scenarios. A future in which she had failed. Did she really need to fear that they would never arrive?

Ragnar was fighting with the weather. He was driving more slowly, as it might be slippery. He had in fact a suitable tread pattern on his tyres, but it was better to be safe than sorry. He cautiously stepped on the brake to test the road. The car reacted entirely normally. No skidding.

'It's not slippery here.'

Ragnar could hardly see anything with the amount of snow that was falling from the sky. He desperately stared at the road in front of him. As a child, he had loved snow. He would romp about with the neighbour's children then and have a snowball fight. How many snowmen had he built? That was fun. Thick socks and gloves were a must otherwise you quickly got ice cold fingers and toes. And they felt numb for a while. What he experienced as odd today was nothing special for the children then.

In winter, people naturally dressed in multiple layers like an onion. A jacket in the outer layer for protection against rain and wind, a warm fleece jacket in the middle and proper underwear inside. That also made taking off clothes easier if necessary. There was usually snow in Iceland; he could be excited about that every year. But now, as a driver, this weather did not have many advantages. Sure, you needed to expect it in autumn but you just hoped that it would not happen.

And as nobody could change the weather, you had to make the best of it. That is why Ragnar bravely drove on. He wanted to keep his good mood.

They crawled at a snail's pace. Suddenly, the windscreen started to steam up.

'Open the window please!' Ragnar said and Annika turned the crank.

'Thanks.'

Gradually, he had a clear view again.

'It's getting too cold in here,' Annika said then.

She turned the crank again and left the window ajar, just a little bit. Then she saw a signpost, it said Geysir.

'Hey, we'll soon be there!'

'Well, it's about time,' Ragnar retorted.

'Hopefully there'll be no more obstacles on the way.'

16

The two finally reached the picturesque place where the Great Geysir and Strokkur could be found without any more incidents. It was situated directly next to the road and even had a petrol station and a hotel next door. They quickly found the car park for the geothermal park. Ragnar parked, and they got out. They were walking along the car park when Ragnar suddenly paused.

'I know this car!' he thought and was appalled. 'It hit us.'

He went around the car and looked at the front. There were dents. It was certain. Or did he only imagine this?

'I wonder who the owner is?' he said. 'Could this be someone from the treasure hunt?'

'Someone doesn't like us,' Annika replied. 'That's scary.'

'Or someone wants to be there first and at all costs,' Ragnar retorted. 'And intimidate us and win.'

'Yes, looks like it,' Annika stated.

'But we can't prove it.'

'Shall we get the police?'

'Oh, that's too much hassle that'll only hold us back. We're late already. We need to take a look here first. They won't be interested in small dents anyway.'

Then they both walked over to the geysers. The landscape looked spooky. Everything was without vegetation because of the steam that came from the ground. The soil was brown and naked. They could hardly see anything, as there was so much steam.

'Where could there be a treasure here?' Ragnar wondered.

'Well, certainly not inside these hot springs,' Annika replied. 'Gee, it stinks here, like rotten eggs.'

It was hard to endure.

'That is sulphur,' Ragnar knew.

The pungent unpleasant smell probably wafted up every visitor's nose immediately. Annika's eyes felt slightly irritated, and she sensed a headache kicking in. She did not want to know what was in this steam, but it was potentially poisonous.

Both of them walked past a few tourists. Every time Annika remained silent for a short while because then she thought automatically, 'NO ONE MUST HEAR!'

But Ragnar kept on talking without concern.

'There is the Great Geysir!'

'And there is Strokkur!'

'Cool!'

They were standing behind the barrier tape watching what happened. Strokkur regularly went off. Approximately every ten minutes. This impressive spectacle attracted many tourists.

Annika was scared. The noise that the geyser made took some getting used to and the fact that boiling hot water was tossed high up into the air was even more threatening. The whole show only took a few seconds and then there was silence again.

'I better leave here,' Annika more or less whispered into Ragnar's ear.

She looked around the giant high temperature field. It was really breath-taking due to its large size. The sky above her was grey and overcast. It could start raining any time or was the rain already over? Ragnar stayed near Strokkur for a while and enjoyed its eruptions. He took photos from all possible perspectives. He had also already photographed the Great Geysir. The sun came eventually out for a last time before the day would be over. Ragnar had followed Annika and was standing behind her. They looked at the mountains in the distance.

'Can you see the snow?' Ragnar asked.

'Yes, it's so beautiful.'

'Did you find anything?'

'No, unfortunately not.'

'Come on, let's go back.'

'I'll take a look at what's over there.'

Annika went to the end of the path and then all the way back the same route and towards the car park. She discovered a sign there. It looked innocent and was advertising walks on the island. It did not stand out among umpteen other signs at all.

They must have passed it by earlier. There was a picture of an impressive waterfall on the sign. It looked exciting with how the water masses outpoured, down from the rock. The inside of the sign was full of thick water drops that the rain must have left. They conveyed a real waterfall atmosphere. Annika centred her attention on the text next to the picture. It read:

Where the water flows
Vigorously down it goes
Look behind, walk under
Get chipper watching a wonder!

'That's Seljalandsfoss,' Annika realised. She wondered where Ragnar was, then saw him.

'I've found it,' Annika cried.

Ragnar read the riddle and said,

'Great. Well done, Annika. That's going to be our next destination then. I'd hoped to find the treasure here.' He tread on the spot. 'But I'm so tired. We'd better not sleep in my car again, it's so uncomfortable. I want a bed.'

'Me, too.'

'Let's see whether the hotel over there still has vacant rooms. Could you go over there and ask please, Annika,' Ragnar suggested. 'I'll go to the car and sort out the luggage.'

'Oh no, please could you ask. Nobody will hear me.'

Annika could not imagine how she should initiate a conversation with a stranger at the reception desk. Addressing strangers without having been asked was incredibly difficult. And when she was speaking, then it was in a low voice. She did not like the sound of her voice. That is how she perceived it. And how could she enter the hotel, greet the strangers and would they be offended easily if she did not show the expected behaviour? And she really worried that the other person would think of her as rude. But all that seemed too complicated and too embarrassing to explain to Ragnar at this point.

'Nobody will hear you?' Ragnar asked. 'Well, I can hear you.'

'Well, and I also don't really know what to say exactly,' Annika said sheepishly.

Of course, she knew how to ask whether there was a vacant room available. In her mind. But the realisation made her tremble inside. There was this paralysing fear again.

'Fine, whatever you want. I'll do it myself,' Ragnar's disappointed reply was.

Annika looked down and she felt hot and dizzy. Surely, she was just getting red like a beet. She always was ashamed of herself in such situations. Why was she unable to do anything? Not even the simplest things such as go and ask something.

As a child, her mother had usually talked for the little Annika and saved her from these troubling inconvenient situations. But as an adult, you just had to be able to do such everyday things yourself and without effort. Then she was overwhelmed by thoughts how she could ever live independently. She promptly got sad and angry at the same time and resolved to act. Something had to change. But how?

Ragnar went to the reception desk and there were indeed several rooms still vacant. In autumn, there were not so many tourists in the interior of the country. And Ragnar booked a room for each of them. Annika was able to charge her phone there later. Ragnar's car remained in the car park all night long. But the other car, the damaged one, was gone in the morning.

17

All participants of the treasure hunt had found the geysers and the new riddle. Helga had driven from the continental bridge to the geysers without delay and she had discovered the sign with the waterfall immediately. She loved hiking and when she walked her dog at home, she enjoyed nature. Sometimes, when her grandchildren visited her, they went for a walk. Then her granddaughter would wear red boots and her grandson blue ones. She liked to buy sweets for her grandchildren but as of late meat was not allowed anymore, as she had changed over to the vegetarian's camp.

She had learnt from a newspaper article that animal fat was unhealthy. The world used to see that differently but since she had health problems she was experimenting with her diet. And she had also read about the suffering of animals in cramped stables and filthy cages and how bad industrial-scale livestock farming was for the environment. That had then been the determining factor for her decision to never touch a piece of meat anymore, even though it had tasted very good in the past.

Gunnar and Jonas had been searching at the geysers at the same time but before Annika and Ragnar arrived. Gunnar had been there before and found it boring to watch Strokkur. He had wanted to see a real volcanic eruption in person. Jonas had heard from foreign passengers in Reykjavik that the geysers were an attraction. Both men had searched everything and had finally found the riddle.

Anton had also been there before Annika and Ragnar and had searched for a long time. A tourist couple asked him to take a photo of them then, directly in front of the sign, and this is how Anton saw the poem by pure chance.

Margret and Oskar saw Sigrun stand in front of the sign. She took a photo. Both thought that she would not do that accidentally and looked at it more closely. They read the sign, and everything was clear. Seljalandsfoss was on their schedule now.

Everyone had found a night's lodging. There was the hotel, a camping site and the possibility to go back to the capital. But nobody wanted to do the latter. There was also overnight accommodation in nearby communities and the south of Iceland was waiting for visitors as well.

The next day, everyone was immediately on the road again. But which one of them would find the treasure first?

18

'Let's go to the waterfall,' Ragnar said when he met with Annika again in the car park the next day as agreed. The sun would rise soon, and they wanted to go to Seljalandsfoss.

The first rays of sunlight blinded Ragnar. Long car journeys were really no fun at all this way. He pulled the sun visor without hesitation and put on his posh black sunglasses. He looked as cool as an action film star.

Ragnar looked over to Annika. His golden hat glittered in the sun.

'Want an apple?' he asked.

Annika nodded. She accepted the apple with thanks.

'I like your hat,' she said suddenly.

'Thank you.'

'Nice and golden, like your car.'

'Yes, that's my favourite colour.'

'Great. Mine is pink.'

'Sure, that's easy to see. You're wearing almost only pink clothes.'

They giggled.

'By the way, I'm a dance instructor,' Ragnar said casually.

'I've mentioned that before, haven't I?'

'Yes, I think so,' Annika retorted.

'Tell me, why were you so weird yesterday when you did not want to go to the reception desk?' Ragnar asked. He furrowed his brow as if he wanted to say that he sometimes found Annika's behaviour mysterious and incomprehensible.

'Well,' Annika sighed. 'Perhaps I'm shy.'

'Perhaps.'

'And certainly with strangers,' Ragnar replied.

No, that was not right. She was not shy.

She just liked to say that because people understood things better that way. But shyness was something very different compared to her situational silence. Shyness could get better with time. It was somehow normal to react insecurely when you first met strangers. But she always had the same problem, and it did not change.

She had to tell him. Her trust in Ragnar had grown enormously over the last few days that they had been on the road together.

'Yes, but it's more than that. I have this problem with talking,' Annika began. 'With communication in general.'

She eventually explained everything to him what she believed that he had to know about her selective mutism and why she was sometimes silent when strangers were nearby.

'Exactly, in certain situations only.'

'Aha,' Ragnar was astonished. 'I've already noticed that you sometimes were suddenly that strangely weird. I'm so sorry if I hurt you. I've never heard of that.'

Ragnar listened very carefully and asked one or two other questions. He also wanted to know what he could do and how he should best behave.

'I'm not cross with you.'

'But good to know. This way, I can help you when you're under stress.'

'Thanks, that's really nice of you.'

'No problem.'

Ragnar had adjusted his expectations. He would accept Annika the way she was and support her if necessary.

'I won't send you to hotels anymore,' Ragnar laughed.

And Annika laughed with him.

19

This time, Annika and Ragnar reached their destination without problems. The waterfall was well signposted and easy to find. And so Ragnar parked his car in the car park.

'Are we here already?' Annika asked in disbelief.

'Yes, it wasn't far,' Ragnar said.

'Come on, let's get out and look around.'

'I've never been here before. I'm curious.'

'Me, too. Only a rainbow is missing.'

'Yes, that would be cool.'

They laughed.

Annika had noted a few facts beforehand. She read them out, 'Seljalandsfoss is a very special waterfall. You can walk along a hiking trail behind the waterfall and then you are basically underneath it. That offers a completely different perspective of the water that is plunging down to the ground. And it provides an interesting adventure for tourists.'

'I like it. I'm totally impressed.'

'I could stand here forever.'

'The waterfall is over 60 metres deep.'

'I've read up on things,' Annika said and laughed.

'Wow!'

'But the path is closed during winter weather. Because it can be slippery, and icicles could fall down so that means it'll be closed today.'

'Darn!' Ragnar exclaimed.

'What are we going to do now?'

'I don't know.'

They looked at each other helplessly.

'Wait a minute.'

'I'll take my camera.'

'Good idea.'

'Zoom in, please. Make it bigger. I can see something there.'

'Where?'
'There's something written. On the wall.'
'I'll read it to you.'
And there was another baffling poem:

> *There is a mountain up close*
> *Its giant size really shows*
> *A dragon lives inside*
> *Fire and ash are in its might!*

20

When Anton arrived at the waterfall, he did not have an eye for the beauty of this wonder of nature. Straightaway he went on not interested in any dangers or prohibitions. He wanted to use the path behind the waterfall but it was cordoned off. Ignoring this Anton just walked on. Nobody saw it and so he would not be punished. But Anton found he was struggling, as the path was really muddy and slippery. He almost fell several times, but he always managed to regain his balance.

'Darn!' he exclaimed.

When he was nearly under the waterfall, he saw the text on the wall in front of him.

'There!' he thought happily.

'The others will never find that one if they are not allowed to go here, ha-ha,' he laughed to himself.

He then went back and got into his car again. That had been easy. He knew it would very soon get more difficult.

21

Granny Helga had also reached the waterfall. But the closure of the path was a big challenge for her. She could not get there. Not with her fragile old bones and you were also not allowed to disregard official notices. She really did not want to get into trouble. How quickly might she break a leg? Or might she be fined if she was caught ignoring the rules?

Actually, she had been fed up the day before already, as she missed her grandchildren so much. She was really looking forward to the little ones' radiant eyes, when she would finally be back again, and she would tell them about her little adventure. To get this far, had been way too exciting. She had had fun, but it was just enough. She was exhausted and the driving was stressful. It was actually not necessary.   She decided to quit the treasure hunt with a heavy heart and drove back home.

Sigrun had made a film at this waterfall years ago, so she knew the place very well. Disappointed about the closure of the path, she remained sitting in her car. When she held her camera towards the waterfall for a photo of a rainbow just above the cascading water the poem appeared very clearly in the background.

Jonas parked his taxi at Seljalandsfoss as well. He always had binoculars with him and he wanted to take a closer look at the waterfall, so he too discovered the poem by chance.

Gunnar soon arrived at the waterfall in his truck. He saw Jonas with the binoculars, and he asked him whether he could borrow them. Jonas gave him the binoculars willingly and so Gunnar also saw what was there.

Margret and Oskar also reached the waterfall at last. They met Gunnar when he was just about to drive on and he immediately told them what they needed to know.

'Don't look far!' he shouted.

He was a good person and happy to help.

And so everyone who was still taking part in the race immediately set off again onto the uncertain way to find this precious treasure.

22

Ragnar and Annika had stayed at Seljalandsfoss for quite a while. They enjoyed the breathtaking view. The water pattered down continuously. The sight could relax you. Or let you dream. Nature really had wondrous surprises to offer and sometimes also special powers and a healing effect for oppressed souls. You could immerse yourself deeply and the world stood still.

Suddenly, there was a rainbow there at the waterfall. It was highly visible from near and far.

'Ah,' Annika exclaimed. 'I had secretly wished for one.'

'Ha-ha,' Ragnar smiled and pushed his golden hat back.

The atmosphere felt really romantic. The air smelled sweet. The colours reflected in the water. Red, orange, yellow, green, blue, indigo, purple. So colourful. As pretty as a rainbow.

'Cool!'

'Strikingly beautiful!'

'I'm happy.'

'I want to dance.'

Ragnar missed his work at the dance studio. He suddenly took Annika's arm and held her by the hand.

And Annika and Ragnar were dancing. They were raising their feet from the ground and spinning around. It felt wonderful.

While doing so, they forgot the treasure hunt and everything else for a moment.

23

Later Annika and Ragnar drove on. The road went straight ahead, further eastbound. They had read the latest riddle accurately and had reckoned that this giant mountain had to be a volcano. It had also mentioned fire and ash. There was indeed no dangerous dragon living inside, but they believed that they had solved the riddle successfully.

'Speaking of dragons,' Ragnar said. 'You know that there's a dragon in the Icelandic coat of arms?'

'Oh, really. Why?'

'It's a land guardian from the legend.'

'Legend?'

'Yes. A long time ago, a foreign king wanted to conquer our land. And he didn't succeed because there were these four courageous land guardians that defended it successfully. In the east, there was a dragon. I believe if I remember correctly in the north, it was an eagle and in the west a bull. And in the south, there was a giant. And that's why all four of them are in the coat of arms.'

'I see. If you say so.'

'Well, but this dragon was surely not meant in the poem. I say it's the volcano.'

And near the waterfall, there was a famous volcano, Eyjafjallajökull. This Icelandic name means as much as the island's mountain glacier, as it is an ice-covered height on the island. This volcanic crater was known for massive ash clouds that it poured out in the past. But now it was not active. This exciting, fire-spitting mountain was over a thousand metres high and neither of them knew whether you could climb it or simply just get near enough to it somehow.

It was getting warmer, and the remaining snow was thawing quickly causing more and more flooding on the road. Rivers from the glaciers of the volcanoes came down from the mountains. The roads were partially flooded but Annika and

Ragnar could drive on for now. Only where else would the journey lead them to?

24

They turned off the main road and went into a narrow side road at the end of which was a car park. There was a coach and several cars. They saw a number of tourists walking in the same direction. So they got out of the car and followed the stream of people towards the mountains. There was a tiny designated path and you could look down into the valley. It was peaceful and quiet down there. They saw a few remote houses, perhaps farmhouses. They climbed on further up. It was very steep. Suddenly, they were standing on the edge of the abyss. Annika felt dizzy. 'Don't fall down,' she thought.

She knew that it was better to stay a little away from the abyss. In case the edge gave way. She also tried to hold tight to something. But there was no handrail on the path; this is why you needed to be careful. Always walk on the inside of the path, not the one facing the abyss. This way it was safe.

Annika and Ragnar enjoyed the fresh air up there. It was cold but the view was great. They could also throw a glance at the glacier ice from afar. It was not clearly visible without binoculars. Then the path seemed to end abruptly or at least it was dangerous to walk on. It would have meant to climb around on very uneven ground. Always with the abyss in mind and the fear of falling down. Nowhere was there a clue to the next destination. There was also no treasure here. So both of them were disappointed and decided to go back to the car.

The way back was easier because both already knew the route. They felt relaxed, were able to look around and took numerous photos. As the path went downhill very steeply for a little bit on the way back, Ragnar suddenly started skidding on some unexpected ice. It had hardly been visible, but it was dangerous. He tumbled but was just able to keep his balance.

He had thoughts of black ice in road traffic. A couple of year ago, he had skidded with his car when he suddenly had to brake. He had not noticed any ice there, but it had nearly caused a severe accident. He would have to walk more carefully.

A few steps further on, it looked even worse on the path. It was slightly covered with snow. Ragnar skidded again and fell. He instinctively put his hands out in front and so they bore the brunt of the impact. His trousers had a hole in them and his knee was bleeding slightly. Annika was completely scared. But she came to his aid and said,

'Oh, that looks really bad. Does it hurt much?'

Ragnar had already got up again in the meantime and had decided that he was not really hurt, and he could walk on.

'It's okay. Thanks,' he said. 'I think my knee's bleeding. I've got a first aid kit in the car, hopefully there's also a plaster for my knee.'

After a pause he went on, 'But these were my favourite trousers.'

'The main thing is nothing is broken,' Annika replied. 'The wrist is prone to that kind of thing. It needs a cast then. One of my classmates once broke his wrist while ice skating. It took a long time to heal and then he couldn't write for months because he couldn't use the hand. I also believe that really hurt.'

'Yes, you're right. It could have been worse. I still have to drive but my hand is fine. And I have other trousers in my luggage,' Ragnar replied.

They walked on. Annika remembered more from her schooldays. She told Ragnar about a trip with her classmates.

'Once, we were at the museum and a child fell.'

Ragnar listened carefully.

'But it wasn't...'

Suddenly, two tourists came in view and Annika was silent in a flash.

'NO ONE MUST HEAR!' she thought.

There was a long silence. Ragnar looked bemused.

'It wasn't, what?' he asked impatiently.

'I must wait until they're gone,' Annika said casually after the strangers had gone away a bit.

'I see.'

Ragnar could not understand that because he had not experienced it himself, but he tried to be nice, as he knew Annika had problems.

'Sorry. I forgot. You'd just explained it to me.'

Every time when they met people on the path, Annika briefly stopped speaking.

But otherwise Annika talked non-stop. She continued,

'But that wasn't bad. There was a nurse at the museum, and she knew immediately what to do.'

'Oh, look, how beautiful the snow is over there!' She pointed to the mountains.

Ragnar nodded in agreement.

Finally, both of them reached the car park again. They searched all around but there was also nothing there. No more clues to help find the treasure.

But where was the treasure?

Annika dug out her phone to research more details on the volcano, but the device's battery was unfortunately already flat.

25

Annika and Ragnar simply decided to drive on. Ragnar felt better. He had found a plaster and his knee had stopped bleeding. It also did not hurt anymore. If it hurt, he would also have painkillers in his bag as a last resort. He did not think about the fall anymore but drove along the road single-mindedly. He had remembered that there had to be a museum somewhere next to the main road. Or was it in the next village?

When the volcano had erupted, there was so much that had been reported in the media. There was global chaos. Planes did not fly anymore because the giant ash cloud posed a potential danger. And afterwards, a few roads needed repair and then he had picked up that there was to be a museum to commemorate the eruption from a newspaper article.

Indeed, they were soon standing in front of the Eyjafjallajökull visitor centre. It was a small house with a giant picture of the eruption of the volcano on the outside wall. You could not miss the visitor centre; it was directly next to the main road. A small car park was adjacent.

'This photo's brilliant,' Annika said when they arrived.

'I also find the forces of nature interesting,' Ragnar answered.

'Are we going to look inside the centre?' Annika asked.

'Why not,' Ragnar replied.

They went inside and learnt a lot about the past eruption. Why were there volcanoes at all? This question had already bothered Annika as a young child, as she was scared of them and perhaps the well explained answer was here. She learnt all kinds of interesting things about the processes in the interior of the earth, continental drifts and plate boundaries.

'Why do they just have to be here in Iceland?'

Nobody could choose where they came from and how it was there. She forgot the thought quickly again because she was on a mission to find the treasure. But there was no clue here as to where it might be. Disappointed, Ragnar and Annika walked around outside in the car park and searched on.

Nothing.

Ragnar had already got into the car again, when Annika suddenly saw a tourist disappear behind the house. He was carrying a black backpack and walked very quickly. He was also holding something in his hand. Annika could not recognise it from a distance. Something black. Was it glittering like metal in the sun?

'Hopefully, that wasn't a weapon, was it?' This thought leapt into her mind at first.

She started to breathe faster.

Her heart pounded and she trembled slightly. Why should someone walk around with a knife or pistol here in this lonely wilderness and hide behind a museum?

It made no sense.

'It can't be.'

Having watched too many films was also not a good idea. Surely, her imagination was playing tricks on her.

'Well, where's he going?' she thought with surprise.

'What's there?'

'I just need to know.'

She followed him carefully and silently and then she was standing at the back side of the house in front of large windows that were decorated with photos of the volcanic eruption. There was lava to be seen and giant ash clouds. She saw the tourist photographing the back of the house using a small, black camera. She breathed a sigh of relief. Her eyes scanned the entire wall. And the ground below as well.

'There's nothing here,' Annika finally thought sadly.

She wanted to go back to the car. She turned around and by chance she looked at an old fence that separated the bordering agricultural area from the visitor centre. It was relatively low and made of metal. Like an animal fence. And there was a sign on it. Very small but it was there. It was hanging forlorn and twisted on this fence. If it had an inscription, it had to be on the other side then because there was nothing written on it.

Annika hesitated.

Was this fence meant for animals? Perhaps it was electrified? Suddenly, Annika was afraid of getting an electric shock.

As a child, she once had touched such an electric fence by accident, and it hurt. She remembered the feeling very clearly. A strange tingling. She did not want to have to experience that again. She could not see any clues that this fence was electric. However, she tried to turn the sign over without touching the fence. She reached out very carefully and turned it around.

And there was indeed something written on it. Black letters on yellowish paper. Laminated for protection against rain. It was tiny but Annika could see it. Annika could hardly believe her eyes. It was a poem. The next task on the way to the treasure. She was absolutely certain. Because it said:

Where the ground is so black
Look for the lava in a stack
Endless expanses of sand to reach
You might find things on the beach!

Evening fell slowly and their night's lodging was a hotel near Skogafoss, another wonderful waterfall in the south of Iceland. You could go very close to the waterfall and take great photos. Annika and Ragnar did not want to miss out on this. They had to pay attention that nothing was icy or snowed-in there, but the weather had been good to them. They only got a bit wet.

Skogar was a gorgeous place. A small village. It was directly at the foot of the island's mountains. There were many hotels in this place, and they had been lucky and had got nice accommodation in one of them. They were in desperate need of a little bit of sleep.

26

Margret and Oskar had also identified Eyjafjallajökull as a possible destination. But where exactly should they look? There was simply no tangible clue. Oskar was quite stressed. He had not brought the right clothing for a walk to a glacier. Margret was usually responsible for packing their bags. She was also stressed because they had not found any clues to the continuation of their journey yet.

'Why didn't you pack my thick jacket?' Oskar moaned.

'How do I know what you want to wear!' Margret retorted.

'Honey, please,' he tried to appease her.

'So, I'm your honey now,' she purred.

'And the grey hiking boots, really!' he grumbled.

'They are at home,' she informed him.

'Great,' he exclaimed sarcastically.

'Do pack your gear yourself!' she shouted.

'Next time I will,' he said a little bit too loudly.

'It would be better that way!' she griped back.

Both had nothing to say anymore to each other for the time being. They remained silent. They were driving along the main road quietly, as they reached the visitor centre.

'Let's look over there,' Margret suddenly shouted abruptly and without remembering the quarrel. It was only just under a quarter of an hour ago.

'Where else?' Oskar snapped.

'Oh, she's talking with me again,' he thought complacently.

'Peace?' he eventually said.

'Peace,' she replied meekly.

They looked at each other shortly and they both laughed. It always was like that between the two, arguing and reconciliation. Very quickly, as if nothing had happened. Like the old couple, that they were. And they stopped and went into the visitor centre. When they were viewing the exhibition, they overheard a conversation between two alleged tourists.

'Have you been outside yet, behind the house, there are great photos!' a stout woman said to a thin man.

'Later. I'm going to look here first,' the man replied.

'Okay,' the woman said.

'Hey Oskar, let's also go and look outside then. I also want to see the photos,' Margret whispered into Oskar's ear.

'Okay,' Oskar reckoned.

When both of them had seen everything inside, they went outside to look. And they were thrilled by the great photos.

'Well,' Oskar mused. 'There's nothing here.'

He held on to the fence and suddenly he saw the sign.

'Margret!' he shouted excitedly.

'Here is something!'

'Come here!'

'Quick!'

Margret came over and when both of them had finally looked closer, they also saw the new riddle in front of them. Sigrun, Jonas, Gunnar and Anton had also come across the sign on the fence. They had looked at the pictures on the house wall. Unfortunately, it was only a poem again, no treasure. They had also made arrangements for the night. They needed sleep. And on the next morning, they were all on their way to the next unknown place, where new surprises were waiting for them.

27

Jonas believed the riddle referred to lava fields. There were many here and they were like a big, endless beach. If you wanted to see it like that. That is why he resorted to the massive lava field next to the road that he had passed by chance. It was hard to move in there, as the lava was very uneven. You could see all sorts of figures; you just had to turn on your imagination. Was this a church? He saw troll children who were hiding behind something in his imagination. Lava formations were interesting for tourists and especially for Jonas right now. The lava presumably originated from an old eruption.

Jonas went further away from the road. He was thrilled. You could easily lose your bearings here, as the lava looked the same all around. He was only wearing light shoes. And the hard stones pierced through his thin soles. The climbing was exhausting but adventurous. Jonas did not care where he stepped. Suddenly, he slipped and fell into a deep hole, which he never expected. His leg was trapped.

'Ouch!' he screamed loudly. Nobody heard him.

But Jonas felt a stabbing pain. He could not move his foot anymore and he also could not walk. He discovered blood on his sock. He trembled and he was in shock about this totally unexpected fall. He felt hot and a little sick. But luckily he had his phone in his pocket. He made an emergency call. And he actually reached someone. He was lucky because the next town was not far away. They sent out an ambulance for him immediately. He tried to keep the leg still. The pain was bearable somehow, but he began to panic when he saw more and more blood. Tear drops rolled down from his eyes and the sick feeling got stronger. And he felt weaker, as he lost a lot of blood.

He closed his eyes and took a deep breath.

'Stay calm,' he said to himself.

He did not move. He waited patiently.

'Please, hurry,' he thought helplessly.

Jonas suddenly remembered an event from his childhood.

He was six years old and home alone because his mother had to leave for a short while unexpectedly. And he was scared. He was playing with his building blocks but suddenly lightning flashed across the sky and the thunder was loud. He hid under the bed in his room and closed his eyes and ears. And he heard a noise, a spooky creaking.

Someone was at the door. Suddenly, it opened and someone exclaimed, 'Where are you?'

Jonas trembled. He did not recognise this voice.

'Are there burglars?' he thought.

The door closed again.

Suddenly little Jonas noticed that he needed to go to the toilet. He tried to hold it in. He was not allowed to wet himself. Mum told him off when he made everything dirty. When the thunder got quieter, he carefully crawled out again from under the bed. He sneaked to the door and listened. It was quiet. He carefully opened the door and had a peek. Darkness. He groped about for the light switch. The light went on and he ran to the bathroom.

When he wanted to go back to his room, he saw a shadow. He ran in the other direction. To the back door. But it was locked. He was trapped. There was no exit. Suddenly, an elderly lady was standing in front of him.

'There you are. Why are you running away from me?'

'I live next door. You know me. Your mother sent me. I'm supposed to look after you, as you're scared of thunderstorms.'

Jonas breathed out. Of course, he knew the lady. He flung his arms around her neck, and he cried.

'No burglars,' he thought with relief.

Now, Jonas was lying there helplessly, and he cried as well. After some time the longed-for help arrived. It had seemed endless to him, but it had just been a few minutes. A paramedic got out and looked at the leg. He felt all around it and asked Jonas all sorts of questions.

'It's probably broken,' he said gently.

'But we'll take you to the hospital just now and x-ray it, then you will know more. You'll be all right.'

He smiled and tapped Jonas slightly on the shoulder. Jonas was pale but thankful for not being alone anymore. The paramedic put a leg splint around his leg and moved him onto a stretcher. Jonas yelped in pain.

'Sorry, it needs to be done, it'll be over soon,' the paramedic explained.

'All right,' Jonas whispered weakly.

Then Jonas got a jab containing a light painkiller. He felt relief, as he could hardly feel his leg now.

Inside the ambulance, Jonas thought,

'I was lucky. I could have died.'

Lava fields can be dangerous. There were invisible voids, and you could fall. That is why you should always have a stick and check the way in front of you to be on the safe side. Or just do not walk around in there at all. And suitable clothing and sturdy shoes would also have been useful. Jonas knew that but now it was too late. That was the end of his treasure hunt.

28

Gunnar drove his truck along the main road at a leisurely pace. He had immersed himself deeply in his music when a small traffic jam suddenly appeared in front of him. He applied the brakes and finally stopped. Traffic just moved forward very slowly. Then he saw, what was there.

'Oh no, a trail of oil,' he thought. 'That's all I needed!'

He had checked and cleaned his tyres only recently. He did not need any contamination. Gunnar waited patiently and only drove on whenever traffic moved on a tiny bit. How long would that take? Anton was also in this traffic jam. He rocked his foot impatiently on the accelerator. Up and down. He could not get on.

'Go now, gosh!'

'Drive on!' he exclaimed angrily.

He gestured impolitely to the driver in front.

'I don't have all day, darn!' he thought.

Slowly, traffic moved on.

Anton hit the accelerator way too heavily. His car started skidding and he only just stopped a few millimetres from the car in front.

Unfortunately, Anton was not the only one in this traffic jam who thought the traffic was not moving on quickly enough. A few cars in front of Anton, there was an accident when two cars crashed together. It looked at first as if it was only damage to the bodywork, but it meant the queue moved even slower. The accident was near Gunnar. He got out of his car to see if he could help.

A lot of oil had leaked, and two cars seemed to have small dents in the bodywork. They must have touched each other only very slightly. Nonetheless, such things were expensive to repair.

'Everything all right?' he exclaimed worriedly.

'Sure, it's not too bad,' a man replied.

'But you can't drive with that anymore.'

The man pointed to the problem.

'Well, the engine had been heavily affected,' Gunnar thought.

'Rather have everything checked out,' he said.

'Luckily no casualties,' another man shouted.

Gunnar automatically looked at the damage more precisely. That ran in the blood of truck drivers.

Two ladies and a child were standing at the roadside. You could see the shock on their faces, but they seemed to be waiting for help. A lady talked to him.

'I believe perhaps, we need a breakdown van.'

'Wait a minute, I know someone I can recommend,' Gunnar offered.

'That would be great.'

He rummaged around in his jacket pocket and eventually gave the lady a business card with the telephone number of a breakdown service. He had used them often; they actually were reliable and quick.

'Here you are, I can highly recommend them,' Gunnar repeated.

'Thank you,' she said.

'No problem, truck drivers are prepared for everything,' Gunnar replied casually.

'Good luck,' Gunnar wished them and said good bye.

Gunnar went back to his truck then. He looked at his vehicle and determined contently that everything was fine. His tyres had survived the incident with the oil unscathed.

Then he drove on.

The traffic jam had also slowly dissolved because the road had been cleaned up in the meantime. Because of that, Anton was ahead and nearly at his destination.

29

Annika and Ragnar had set off again. They wanted to go to the black beach Reynisfjara that was in the south of the isle near the fishing village Vik. The inhabitants of the village were prepared for tourists. Here, you could eat and buy gifts. On their way to Vik, neither had noticed the oil on the road or the accidents. The road was clear, and they enjoyed being together in the car. Horses and sheep were eating with relish on both sides of the road.

They were there. The wind was blowing a bit stronger on the beach. But the sea was calm. There was also a playground with monkey bars, swings, a seesaw and a sandpit. There were hardly any people there, but both saw a family. The father had written something in the sand with his finger. The mother took a photo of it.

The children had built a small sandcastle, directly next to the writing. The castle had four high towers on each corner. The entrance gate was clearly visible. The walls looked stable from afar. The little boy had a blue toy shovel in his hand and was eagerly digging a hole. That eventually became a moat all around the building. Then he took his green bucket and ran to the water. The full bucket got tipped out after that. His sister was playing with colourful plastic shapes.

'Give me the fish, please!' she heard the boy say.

'Here you are. We still need knights,' the girl said.

'Yes, and fish in the moat.'

'Yes!'

Annika heard the children laugh. They ran merrily around their work and giggled.

'Look, Mum!' the boy shouted proudly.

The mother took another photo and smiled.

'Well done, Toni!'

'We need to move on,' Annika heard the father say.

'I'm hungry,' the girl exclaimed.

'Me too,' the boy said.

When the family left the beach a little later, Annika went to the sandcastle. The writing was still readable, 'Fun at the Beach'.

'You'd want to be this cheerful,' she thought with grief.

Ragnar had come close to her and had also seen the work of art.

'Cool,' he said.

'Oh, I'd like to be in a real castle now,' Annika daydreamed.

'Yes, me too.'

'With you!'

'You're my princess,' Ragnar fooled around.

'And you're my prince.'

They laughed.

After a moment of silence, Annika finally said,

'Well, the poem definitely led us to the beach. And now?'

'We need to search,' Ragnar answered.

'We have no other choice.'

'That's right.'

'You go to the left and I go to the right. We'll meet back here at the sandcastle, in a quarter of an hour,' Ragnar said. 'Or better what's left of it.'

'Okay. See you,' Annika agreed while smiling and walked away.

Ragnar looked at the sea for a while and daydreamed. There were striking rocks to be seen. Legend had it that they could be trolls. Or were they rather relics of an old ship? Anyway, Ragnar thought they were great. He stared at the water as if he was under a spell.

'If only I were a fish, easy-going and free,' he thought.

Then he went on. The black sand crunched under his feet. A wave suddenly came very close to him.

Annika stayed far away from the water, as she was scared of the big waves. The beach could be dangerous here. You never knew when a wave that was a little stronger than expected would come. Accidents must certainly have happened here before. Unfortunately, there was no sign of another clue. The treasure was far away at the moment.

30

Sigrun had reached the beach. She was just standing there looking around. Where should she look for a treasure or a clue? She was at a loss. As an actress, she had often been allowed to visit interesting places, as film sets are usually also selected because of their beauty. Sigrun walked up and down the beach. She sat down and put her hand into the sand. Her fingers felt each single grain. The sand felt cold. But she experienced it as pleasant.

'Oh, it's beautiful here,' she thought.

And she began to breathe deeply. She looked at the water. Daydreaming calmly was just good.

'I could sit here forever.'

'But I have to find a clue.'

She closed her eyes and imagined the treasure.

It was a giant chest with a golden lock. And she had the key. It was heavy and decorated with gold. She had the honour to open the chest. She proudly put the key in the lock. And she turned the key. Very slowly. Once. And once again. And then she took her hands and slowly lifted the lid of the chest. She opened up the chest and then she finally saw the treasure.

The chest was full of gold and silver. There were necklaces and rings, bangles and bracelets. A golden crown with sparkling red gems especially caught her eye. The rubies were simply splendid. Then she saw gemstones in all colours. Earrings with blue sapphires and a brooch with a wonderful green emerald. It was a feast for the eyes. She was rich now! And famous. The proud treasure finder! Suddenly, something shone in her eyes. A bright light had dazzled her, and it had ripped her out of her daydream. Using her hands, she covered her eyes and opened them slowly again.

'Alas, no treasure here,' she thought disappointedly. 'Go now, I need to search.'

She got up and went to the rocks on the verge of the beach. She had been there. But there was absolutely nothing.

'I'll give up,' she thought groggily.

'There's no point in that.'

Suddenly, she saw Annika. She was wandering alone along the beach.

'Hey, did you find anything?' she shouted over to her.

Annika seemed to be frightened. But she did not answer.

'Is she ignoring me?' Sigrun thought and she was baffled. 'Or did she not understand me?'

So Sigrun went closer and asked again.

Annika shook her head.

'No.'

'Well, I'm going to give up,' Sigrun said.

'There's nothing here.'

They both walked on together. Ragnar had walked in the opposite direction for a bit in the meantime and had returned. He had not found anything either. Now he saw Annika and Sigrun with their heads down. He was sure, they had also found nothing.

The three of them met and thought about what they could do.

'Go home?' Sigrun reckoned.

'No, that's not worth it,' Ragnar retorted.

'Now, that we made it this far.'

'You're right,' Sigrun said.

Annika stood there silently. She stared at the sea and felt sad.

'The water is certainly ice cold,' she thought.

Suddenly, she noticed something. She went closer and saw it was an old bottle.

'Who's throwing all the rubbish into the sea,' she thought angrily.

But then she saw something in there.

'A message in a bottle,' she thought.

She grabbed the bottle and tried to open it. Unfortunately, without success. So she went back to Ragnar and Sigrun. Both of them were surprised and thrilled.

Ragnar was able to open the old bottle with an effort and he pulled out a note.

'Wow,' Sigrun exclaimed.

'I don't believe it!'

It was really a genuine message in a bottle.

And it said on the note:

The glacier becomes a lake
Progress you make
Drivin' or swimmin'
You need to determine!

'Oh, Annika, you're as good as gold,' Ragnar exclaimed.

And Sigrun agreed with him.

'Awesome!'

Annika beamed. She was also a little ashamed because she was suddenly the centre of attention. But at the same time, she was glad that she had found the next clue.

Ragnar put the note back into the bottle and placed it back on the sand.

'For the others,' he said.

'Let's give them a chance.'

Annika nodded silently. She knew the solution.

'Okay,' Sigrun said reluctantly.

'That's what you do with a message in a bottle, otherwise a bad curse lurks.'

'Where did you get that from?' Ragnar asked and smiled.

'Well, isn't it always like that in films?' Sigrun replied insecurely.

'With pirates,' Ragnar thought in amusement, but he did not say anything anymore.

31

Anton had seen Sigrun, Annika and Ragnar in the car park. And he had tried to work out from their behaviour where they had to go next.

'I certainly won't make my shoes dirty and everything full of sand. Go on now, follow them. They will lead me to the destination,' he thought, self-satisfied. He felt very smart and always a tiny step ahead of the others.

Gunnar had also reached the beach. He immediately saw the bottle.

A message in a bottle?

'No, that isn't from a sunken ship, is it?' he thought with surprise.

He opened it and read it.

Margret and Oskar came to the beach just as Gunnar was reading the note. So they could also read the poem. Gunnar was not cagey about it. He then put the note back into the bottle and very carefully threw the bottle back into the water in case, anyone else was still looking for the clue. And also as a matter of principle.

'It will get washed ashore again and then the next one will find it and be happy,' Gunnar announced, solemnly.

'A pirate treasure,' Oskar joked.

'Exactly,' Margret laughed.

The three were satisfied and went on their way again.

32

Annika and Ragnar had stopped at a lava field. They had to take a look at this whatever. They had not noticed anything about the misfortune that had befallen to Jonas. Annika was careful like she always was.

'I can't walk along there,' she said to Ragnar.

'That's too risky for me.'

'And it's impossible with these shoes on.'

Ragnar stood at the side.

'Yes, I'm just going to look from the side.'

'It's really cool, isn't it?'

'Absolutely.'

'I have never seen such a thing at close range.'

'Me neither.'

'These are the miracles of Iceland,' Ragnar joked and held tight his golden hat because it was a little windy and he did not want it to get blown away.

'Yes,' Annika said in agreement.

Suddenly, it started raining and Annika and Ragnar got into their car again quickly. Anton had secretly followed Annika and Ragnar. He had watched them both. He had also stopped at the lava field but so far away that they did not notice. Now he was sitting in his car impatiently thinking, 'Hurry up, guys!'

He was disappointed when they got into their car again after a short time without having gone anywhere at all. So, the treasure could not be hidden in the lava field.

'They just must have stopped for some fresh air,' Anton believed.

As the car in front of him drove on again, he continued his pursuit without attracting attention.

33

Annika and Ragnar suddenly felt hungry at the same time. They were now in the national park Vatnajökull. This is the biggest national park in Iceland and among other things it consists of the glacier named Vatnajökull, which means water glacier in translation. It originated over 2,000 years ago. Its area is more than 8,000 square kilometres. Nearly half of that is ice. But due to the climate changes of our time, the glacier is shrinking more and more. Furthermore, there are a few active volcanoes in this area below the glacier. And the heat is making the ice melt.

'Where could there be a shop here for us to buy food?' Ragnar asked sarcastically.

'Well, where is the next village?' he kept on asking.

'No idea.'

'There's nothing here,' Annika said. 'In this lonely wilderness.'

'Until we reach the glacial lagoon, there's not much along the route anyway,' Annika determined soberly after a look at the map.

'There might be a gift shop there that sells snacks,' Ragnar said full of hope.

'And another clue to where we will find the treasure,' Annika reckoned.

'Yes, of course.'

'Too bad, that we've run out of food now.'

'Sorry,' Ragnar said.

'I forgot to get something yesterday.'

'Never mind,' Annika griped.

It could actually happen to anyone. They had fallen into their beds immediately the evening before, absolutely exhausted, and had fallen asleep.

'We won't starve to death.'

They both laughed.

'We'll be there soon.'

'Well, let's hope so.'

There was something lying on the road. It looked like a dead animal that had been run over. They could not recognise much of what it used to be.

'Oh...'

'Now I'm not hungry anymore,' Annika said.

'Me neither,' Ragnar replied.

They laughed again but this time, it was not really funny.

34

Annika and Ragnar eventually reached the glacial river lagoon Jökulsalon. Because of its beauty, it has also been nicknamed the crown jewels of Iceland. There are fascinating sheets of floating ice and massive icebergs on the lake. You can see and admire them from afar.

The lake developed when lumps of ice detached themselves from the glacier and fell into a valley below. The lagoon developed because of the warmth, and it is nearly 300 metres deep. It is now many times bigger than just 40 years ago and is continuously growing. Lumps of ice floating in the water have different shapes. Some are up to 15 metres high. Sometimes they fluoresce in blue because of the reflections on the ice crystals or in black because of the volcanic ash.

Annika and Ragnar had understood from the last clue that they had to keep on searching here. Of course, it was not clear at all again, where exactly. Annika only knew that you could explore the glacial lake with a special vehicle that could drive on land and in water. Tourist groups got invited to try it and it sounded exciting.

This amphibian vehicle was already an attraction in itself. It had a body like a ship but also wheels like a car. There were several of these here. And such a vehicle could transport quite a lot of tourists; it was large like a truck. One of them was on the move on the lake at the moment, another one was standing at the car park, almost empty, and a few visitors were just getting off. These vehicles were yellow like these well-known American school buses.

'Oh, that looks like it was made for a cool film scene,' Ragnar exclaimed.

'Yes, films have been made here already,' Annika answered.

'Oh, really? Which ones?'

'James Bond and so on,' Annika enlightened him.

'Oh, cool.'

'Let's take a look around here,' Ragnar said.

They both got out of the car and went for a walk. It was good to stretch their legs after such a long drive. Ragnar had a stretch.

'It's cold here,' Annika reckoned.

'Yes, what do you think, that's ice!'

'Look, there,' Ragnar exclaimed and pointed in the direction of the lake.

Now she saw it, too. There was ice everywhere. She put on her scarf, hat and gloves. Now the cold could not harm her.

'Come on now,' she said.

'I'm ready.'

Unfortunately, there was no shop that sold food. Merely, a small house with picnic tables in front of it was visible. They would have to stop in the next big town.

Only an Icelandic flag was blowing on a pole in the wind. It was blue with a white cross and a red cross inside the white cross.

Annika and Ragnar spontaneously decided to go on the boat tour. Simply out of curiosity. Perhaps the treasure was lying in the lake? They had to put on an orange life vest and were then allowed to get on the amphibian vehicle together with many others. It drove off slowly, first of all on land. Everything was wobbling. Then it moved towards the lake and eventually its lower part disappeared into the water. It was floating quite calmly. The visitors were astonished and pulled out their cameras. Ragnar and Annika were also amazed. The sheets of ice were breathtaking. And the play of colours in the prevailing lighting conditions was really great. Seals emerged from the lake and descended again, and some others were lying around on the further away sheets of ice.

'So romantic here,' Ragnar whispered into Annika's ear. He was smiling.

She nodded hardly noticeably.

Annika made an effort to take lots of photos. At the same time, she watched vigilantly to see if there was a clue to the treasure somewhere here.

But she could not find anything.

35

Anton had stayed behind Annika and Ragnar until they reached the lagoon. They had not noticed.

'I see, the glacial lagoon,' he thought. 'Of course. I'll let them find the treasure and then I'll collect it from them.'

'Ha-ha!' he laughed with satisfaction.

He saw how Annika and Ragnar got on the vehicle.

'That will take some time,' he thought.

He was tired, so he took a quick nap in his car. He closed his eyes and fell asleep. A little later, pedestrians heard a loud snore.

Meanwhile, Gunnar, Sigrun and Margret and Oskar had also arrived at the lagoon. They had the same idea as Annika and Ragnar; they wanted to go on the tour. And so everyone ended up on this vehicle in an orange life vest. It was not comfortable but would keep them safe.

When the tour was finished, the sky was dark. It was even colder now than before. Annika and Ragnar got in their car because it was so cold, and he switched on the heating. He also let the engine run.

'That was great but what are we going to do now?' Ragnar said.

Annika shrugged. 'But it's nice and warm here. I need that now,' she smiled.

Then she looked up to the waving flag on the pole next to the house by chance. The wind was moving it gently up and down. Suddenly, she paused.

'There's something there,' she said to Ragnar. 'Is there anything written on it?'

Ragnar looked up to the flag in bewilderment.

'Yes, you're right. There's something written on it.'

'Weird, is that the clue?'

'Come on, let's get closer.'

Anton was sitting a few metres away from them in his car watching them. He had just woken up shortly before they came back.

'What are they doing there?' he thought, totally confused.

Annika and Ragnar got out again and went closer to the flag.

Now Annika could recognise it clearly.

There was another poem.

> *By the fjords in the East*
> *No ferry costs, at least*
> *Just look at the port*
> *And success will not fall short!*

After the boat tour, the other treasure hunters had decided to explore more of the location. The car park was large, and it was possible to take a closer look at a giant bridge over the main road. It spanned the water. But there was no treasure near the bridge either. As they were coming back to the car park disappointedly, they saw Annika and Ragnar standing next to the flag. Both of them looked up very obviously and the text stuck out like a sore thumb to everyone now.

Anton had also watched the events unfold and he had now seen the message, too.

'Let's go to the ferry,' he thought and left the car park in a hurry.

36

Annika and Ragnar had also set off again. They were going further eastward. They had decided to go shopping in the next place that they came to along the way and they also wanted to sleep somewhere. They had to turn off the ring road. The place was called Höfn and it was very beautiful. There was also a supermarket where you could buy anything. Ragnar had certain ideas.

'We need bread and cheese!'

'And Skyr.'

This Icelandic dairy product was very similar to yogurt. It was particularly delicious with custard flavour or fruits.

'Do you have a spoon?'

'I always have cutlery in my luggage.'

'Very good!'

There were a few restaurants at the harbour. You could eat fresh fish or lamb. But tourists did not often stumble into them by accident because they were relatively expensive.

Suddenly, Annika saw a dog. All alone and without a leash. Nobody was to be seen. Who could be the owner? It had brown fur that looked unkempt. But she could not say what breed it was. Anyway, it appeared to be quite big to Annika and it was barking loudly. That made it even bigger in her eyes. It had to be a stray. She could not tell whether it had any dangerous illnesses. Dogs also have teeth.

Annika had been really scared of dogs since she was a young child. She had never had close contact with a dog but the dangerous stories that her mother told her were more than enough to give her a fear of dogs. Perhaps her mother had experienced something bad with dogs; she talked about it without end saying that dogs would bite. Annika did not know that for sure. After all, her mother was an expert for the depiction of any actually existing and invented dangers of all kinds, why that was the case, nobody knew. Perhaps it was in the genes. Annika had always felt immediately how her heart started beating faster when she saw unknown dogs in the park.

'What if it jumps at me,' she thought worriedly.

She wanted to avoid it but it came directly towards her.

'Darn,' she just thought.

But it was too late. The dog was almost standing directly in front of her. It wagged its tail and barked even louder. Annika cringed. What did this dog want from her? She wanted to scream. But she saw pedestrians from the corner of her eyes.

'NO ONE MUST HEAR!'

She could not scream. The dog came closer and closer and stopped a few centimetres in front of her. It was still barking. Instinctually, Annika wanted to run away but she stood rooted to the spot.

Then a passer-by stepped in. It was an elderly lady wearing a striped coat. Annika had not noticed that the lady had been close by all the time.

'This cute pug won't harm you, love,' she said.

She made a move and thereupon the dog backed off.

It had quickly found a new thing that aroused its interest. A restaurant worker had just brought scraps. Certainly, there were small bones in them. The dog ran away fawning towards the bin.

The lady looked worriedly at Annika.

'It's gone,' she said and then she went on shaking her head.

Annika was standing there alone again, and she was shaking. That was a close thing. She felt ashamed. A tear drop ran down her cheek. Why was she afraid of a cute pug? It had appeared to her like it was a giant wolf.

And why was she unable to call for help?

37

Sigrun felt a slight pain. She had arrived in Höfn a while ago. The scenery was beautiful here and she wanted to go to the water immediately. There were many small fishing boats at the harbour. It was a quaint village and the air smelled like the sea.

She had found a parking space at the roadside and had got out of her car. And then her tooth suddenly hurt.

'Oh dear,' she thought. 'What am I going to do now?'

She should have had it taken care of months ago. After eating it hurt more and more and it was keeping her awake at night. But now, the pain came very unexpectedly.

It came and went.

She tried to ignore it.

There was so much to see here. A boat went out onto the sea. Its sails swayed slowly in the wind. Sigrun took a deep breath and felt the salty sea air more intensively. Then the dragging pain in her tooth came back. She pondered whether she would find a dentist here. She was not very familiar with this area. She walked through the streets aimlessly and looked into the windows of the houses. She saw colourful roofs and fences then the pain reappeared. Worse than ever before. And she also had a headache.

Bright light dazzled her eyes and intensified the pain. She wanted to scream. But she put her sunglasses on and walked on bravely. Then she was overcome by strange feelings of weakness and severe dizziness. She held on to a house wall. It soon got slightly better. She noticed a sign that indicated a medical facility. She went in and indeed discovered that there was also a dentist. Sigrun enquired whether Doctor Petursson could give her emergency treatment. And she was lucky indeed.

As another patient had cancelled his appointment, she did not have to wait for long at all. When she was sitting in the waiting room, she felt this dull headache again. But when she entered the treatment room, it was gone again. The dentist drilled the tooth carefully and filled out the hole with a substance. Sigrun felt exhausted but the tooth finally did not hurt anymore.

Back in the street, she felt the fresh wind. She took a deep breath in and returned to her car. It was still there where she had parked it and the varnish was shining. The car was not new, but it was useful.

Sigrun drove to her hotel room in Höfn that she had booked beforehand, and she went to bed. Taking a shower had to be cancelled and she was also not hungry. Her head was hammering like mad. She just wanted to sleep but that was of course not possible on cue. But she enjoyed the silence and the darkness that the curtains gave her. After a while, she eventually fell asleep.

When she woke up the next morning, the headache was unbearable. When she moved, she felt sick. She knew that was her migraine. She got such bouts every now and then, especially under stress. And this treasure hunt was stressful.

She would certainly spend the next few hours in bed with her eyes closed. And hours could quickly become days. She needed a lot of rest now. Her head would burst in the car. It was over. Sigrun had to give up the treasure hunt with a heavy heart.

38

Annika and Ragnar had stocked up on new provisions in Höfn and found rooms for the night. In the morning, they drove on. The latest riddle obviously sent them to Seyðisfjörður, the place where the ferry to the European mainland departed. The incident with the dog had already been forgotten.

They came to beautiful fjords. Several of these narrow arms of the sea were located directly in front of them. The road wound along at one side first and then back again at the other side. Most of the time, they saw the sea. The water was calm but it looked beautiful.

'I'd like to live here,' Ragnar said. 'Always being near water and having a boat would be best.'

'Sounds great,' Annika replied.

'Going on little excursions and letting the sea breeze caress your face,' Ragnar continued dreamily. 'And in addition, perhaps a garden to grow vegetables and lovely flowers.'

Annika smiled.

Then she said quietly, 'Let's dream.'

Ragnar also smiled. At this moment, all seemed right with the world for both of them.

But then they got into a traffic jam, there must have been an accident because the road was flooded. There must have been a heavy downpour which they had not noticed.

'Oh, no,' Ragnar sighed.

Annika was also not a happy bunny. 'Why does this always have to happen to us?' she thought sadly.

But gradually the traffic moved forward. A bend was obviously lying ahead. The drivers slowly saw what exactly was going on there. A few vehicles were stuck in water. The wheels were hardly visible. Mud from the road had mixed with the water. Half of the road was unusable. A police car was also to be seen. Annika asked herself whether this was dangerous. She tried not to look.

Meanwhile, Ragnar slowly drove on. He had to concentrate on the road, as the passage was quite narrow. But they were able to drive past without problems.

'It wasn't too bad,' Ragnar said casually.

He had not seen much of the obstacle, but he was an optimist. At least, most of the time. And then the traffic jam was over, and everyone could drive on normally, as if nothing had happened.

'Sometimes it's that quick,' Ragnar said.

Annika smiled again.

39

Annika and Ragnar drove on, further east.

Suddenly Annika shouted, 'A reindeer!'

'There's a reindeer!'

In the area around Seyðisfjörður, there were reindeers, indeed. Most of them were more or less brown. Their fur was shiny. These animals had powerful antlers. The male ones were stronger than the females. The mountains around the place were quite high and snow-covered. Reindeers love snow, as they can find food in there. They are resistant to the cold and have stamina.

'That's so beautiful,' Annika exclaimed.

'And already gone again,' Ragnar said.

Because they had already passed it.

'Hope we get to see another one!'

'They are quite nice there, but I don't want them in front of my car!'

'Oh, yes. I think they're great when they help Santa,' Annika said.

'Rudolph, with his red nose.'

'Yes, but I believe reindeers don't have red noses at all, do they?'

'No idea. I don't think so.'

Neither of them were reindeer experts.

'But there were a few other reindeers with Santa,' Ragnar suddenly reckoned.

'What were they called again?'

'Oh. Let me think.'

'The ones that pull the sleigh.'

'Yes, because Santa needs to get ahead quickly.'

'I've seen that in a film, it was so cool.'

'Donner. Blitzen. Dasher and Prancer,' Annika said.

'Vixen.' Ragnar mulled over it intensely. He frowned.

'Exactly. And there's one missing?'

'Dancer.'

'Yes, and Comet.'

'I believe there were nine.' Annika was not sure.

'And Cupid, too,' Ragnar exclaimed.

'Right. That could be all of them,' Annika reckoned.

'One moment,' she hesitated.

Annika listed them all.

'Donner, Dasher, Prancer, Blitzen, Vixen, Comet and Cupid, Dancer and Rudolph, of course. Yes, there are nine.'

'Oh, I wish it was Christmas today,' Ragnar mused.

'At home with delicious food. Candlelight and Christmas tree.'

'Speaking of food,' Annika laughed.

She reached out for her bag. Annika was hungry and she had bought something very special at the supermarket. The sandwich with reindeer meat tasted very delicious. Annika liked to eat when the car was in motion. She was chewing.

The view out of the window was not boring. There was the water and high mountains. Directly next to the road, there was running water. The sight was somehow romantic. Small trees and bushes were mirrored in the water. But she did not see any more reindeers. Then an occupied area came in view.

'Finally there,' Ragnar said contentedly. His golden hat was shining.

But where was the treasure or a clue to find it hidden?

40

Seyðisfjörður, the fjord of the fireplace, was a small community with a picturesque harbour in the east of Iceland. The car ferry from Denmark arrived here and it brought a multiplicity of tourists to the island. Some people were on a round trip with their cars and went back home again by boat later. That was an interesting way of exploring Iceland.

Annika and Ragnar were glad to be there, finally. The first houses appeared to the left and to the right. They were fairly ordinary. There was a car park with tourist information, a map of the place and numerous photos of the area behind glass in display cases. Trees had carefully been planted in a row. The people of this place seemed to know how to welcome visitors.

'Nice here,' Annika said.

'Yes, that's a lovely reception. I'm going to the harbour, then we'll see,' Ragnar said determinedly.

The road led them further on and finally they reached the harbour building. They saw a big space with several long lanes and a custom house. Vehicles could queue up for the ferry there.

But everything was empty.

To the left and right, water was to be seen. Then they saw a big ship.

'Look, the ferry is coming!' Ragnar exclaimed with excitement.

The giant white ship was sitting there in front of them majestically. Annika counted four floors with tiny windows. It was like a city on the water. She saw the black chimney and the lifeboats alongside. But she could not recognise any people.

Snow-covered mountains were still in the background. A petrol station advertised using a big banner. The place seemed like an idyllic village. There was a church, a hotel, several shops. The houses were made of wood, mainly grey and brown.

They found accommodation by the water. The room was equipped with every feature that you could wish for on a treasure hunt. A picture with golden yellow sunflowers was hanging on the wall. Ragnar was in the shower and enjoyed the jet of water.

Annika had disappeared into bed quickly. Since she had been out and about she slept much better. The reason must have been the exciting adventures away from home. She was simply completely exhausted each evening.

On the next day, both of them were outside again. They saw birds. Puffins. They were flying around so elegantly and effortlessly.

'Being so carefree would be great,' Annika thought.

'Free like a bird.'

Her thoughts remained unspoken. Ragnar thought the same. But he also kept quiet.

Both of them searched the harbour thoroughly. The ferry came from far away and quickly disappeared again. Thus, it was unlikely that something was on it. The treasure would not directly lie in the street, would it? Or would there just be a new riddle again? But there were artefacts. Monuments. Annika saw a huge propeller in front of a house. It is also called a ship's screw. Hard to imagine that such a massive thing once moved boats.

She examined the object but there was nothing to discover. Suddenly, Ragnar shouted that there was something there. Behind another house, there was a giant anchor. Annika ran around it and looked. From above. From the side. From below.

Nothing. She saw the curved ends of the anchor that used to hold boats at the bottom of the sea. She imagined that to be very adventurous. When Ragnar called her again, she suddenly turned around.

'Oh, there is a display board here,' Annika remarked then.

Interesting details about the anchor could be read there. And there was the next clue.

Further northbound like the wind
You really must obey this hint
A waterfall is coming along
Dettifoss is big and strong!

41

'Well Dettifoss,' had been Ragnar's reaction to the riddle.

Annika had already informed herself and was now reading to Ragnar what she had found out about it.

'Dettifoss is one of the most powerful waterfalls in Europe. It is 100 metres wide, and its water appears to be greyish white. The water drops 44 metres down into the depth. That is the reason for the name Dettifoss, which means collapsing waterfall.'

'Oh, interesting,' Ragnar reckoned and prepared the car.

Both of them wanted to drive to the waterfall immediately but Annika had had too much to drink and needed the loo urgently. She tried her luck at the harbour buildings and found what she was looking for. On her way back, she noticed that something was moving between the cars. It was fast and she could not tell what it was from a distance.

Was it a defenceless animal? Did it need help, as it could get run over anytime? She decided to take a closer look. Ragnar could wait for a minute longer. The animal had gotten itself onto a nearby greenspace. Plants hid the view. It appeared to be in trouble.

'Perhaps it is injured?' Annika thought.

When she came closer, she heard a quiet hiss.

'Don't be scared, little one,' Annika said quietly. No human being was there.

'I want to help you.'

She hoped that her trembling voice would not give away that she was scared herself. Annika kept on going slowly and quietly. A black and white tail was moving through the air.

'Meow!'

Finally, she found a kitten in the grass. The animal was unkempt, but she could not see any injuries at first sight. Surely it was hungry. The cat slowly sneaked around Annika and purred. Annika's heart was beating rapidly. Her hands trembled. But she smiled at the cat.

'Calm down. Everything is fine,' she whispered to herself.

Contrary to dogs, cats were not really frightening for Annika. She actually found them quite cute. Every child did have a favourite animal even if their mother would not allow pets. Annika had always dreamt of having a fluffy friend. She did not move. What should she do now? She plucked up all her courage, took a deep breath and picked up the cat. She quickly ran back to the car.

Distracted by the cat, Annika did not look at the ground in front of her. She missed a puddle and her feet got wet. The cold reached her toes.

Then she did not notice that a small stone was lying on the path. Annika tripped. She just managed to avoid a fall, but her sole got detached. The shoe was definitely broken. Unfortunately, she had not taken any spare shoes with her.

How should she walk to the waterfall now?

42

In many places, the ground was dirty and muddy. Annika absolutely needed reasonable footwear. She decided to obtain new shoes immediately. She wanted sturdy shoes that were suitable for walking. And Annika imagined the perfect pair. Black ones would be best. Shiny leather. And super comfortable. And the shoes should also smell good, please.

Once Annika had bought boots made of plastic. It was simply impossible to get rid of the chemical smell. She was unable to wear these boots at all. She had tried to alleviate the stench in the fresh air but to no avail. Eventually, they ended up in the bin.

She had also not dared to claim a refund. For unused, not useable boots. Good thing they had not been very expensive. Well, they were pretty. Anyway, she knew now that she had to be completely sure that she really found the right shoes. Did she not see a shoe shop in the town the day before? She showed the broken shoe to Ragnar.

'Well, go and buy new ones quickly,' was his terse reaction and he drove Annika to the said shoe shop later.

Ragnar's reaction to the cat was fiercer.

'Annika! What are we supposed to do with a cat? We are on a treasure hunt. Surely it has an owner somewhere here.'

But Annika insisted, the cat had to come along.

Just in case, Ragnar went to the harbour building again and asked whether anyone missed a cat. A worker said the stray had appeared a while ago.

'Perhaps off of the boat from Denmark! Nobody knows what kind of stuff comes from there, really!'

The residents from neighbouring houses assured him that they did not have a cat. Allegedly, no cat was missing in town. And it was a long way to go to the next place.

Annika sat in her seat and stroked the cat. Her hands went gently through its soft fur. Annika found that relaxing. The cat obviously enjoyed it as well.

'It needs a name,' Ragnar reckoned.

'Felix.'

'That is a proper cat's name,' Annika confirmed.

'Besides, he's a male cat.'

'Yes.'

'Ha-ha.' Both laughed.

Then Annika had to go to the store. She had decided to do so on her own and to pick nice shoes. Ragnar could look after the tomcat in the meantime. Felix, the lucky one.

Annika opened the door of the store tentatively. Her heart pounded.

'Okay, take a deep breath,' she thought.

She sharply pulled the air in through her nose and out again through her mouth. The out breath took a little longer.

'And go!' She entered.

There was no one to be seen.

There were shoes everywhere. There was a shelf with trainers there and one with elegant shoes for gentlemen. Most of them were dark, black or brown. She noticed colourful children's shoes and around the corner there were shoes for ladies. The air smelled of leather and vanilla. Apparently, someone had tried to create a pleasant atmosphere for shopping using air fresheners. Soft music played in the background. There was no singing, she only heard a guitar. Annika remembered the tune, but she could not think of what it was.

Annika looked around and went to a shelf with shoes in her size. She took a pair that she liked. She examined the shoes all around, sat down and tried a shoe on. It fitted like a glove. The other one fitted as well.

'Yes, these ones are good,' she thought happily.

'And how much are they?' That was her next thought.

But the price was nowhere to be seen. Annika got frightened. There was no sales personnel in sight. She saw other customers with a child next to the slippers aisle.

Then she finally spotted a shop assistant at the till. She seemed loud and wore a dark blue dress with flashy silver clasps. There was something terrifying about her. Everything in Annika instinctively refused to come into contact with this woman. Yet Annika noticed even more that stopped her from doing so. There were several customers queuing and someone was paying for a pair of black boots. She could not just go and ask what the shoes cost because

'NO ONE MUST HEAR!'

She desperately searched the shelf, looked at the shoes and the box several times. But there was simply no price there! Annika panicked. She also did not know whether she had enough money with her. What if not? Perhaps she should get help from Ragnar?

Lost in thought, the shoes in her hands, Annika walked in the direction of the exit. Suddenly, she heard a sharp voice shouting from behind her.

'Hey, young lady, where are you going with these? Do you think these shoes don't cost anything!'

Frightened, Annika stared at the shop assistant. She froze. Was she a thief now?

She felt hot and dizzy. It was as if her heart was about to burst. She wanted to defend herself, but she could not say anything.

'NO ONE MUST HEAR!'

'Cat's got your tongue?' the shop assistant nagged on.

The shop assistant and the other customers stared at Annika in amazement.

It must have been seconds.

Endless silence.

The lump in her throat made her feel helpless.

She wanted to sink into the ground. Drop dead.

Anything was better than this infinite shame.

She suddenly pictured herself in a striped suit behind bars. Trapped forever, just because she could not talk. Laughed at and tortured. Dead. But her heart kept on beating. Suddenly, she had the saving idea. She pointed with her finger at a mirror that stood by the exit.

The shop assistant understood.

'Oh sure, feel free to look at yourself. These shoes are sure to look good on you. And they are on offer today only, as it says on the sign there!'

The shop assistant turned back to the other customers.

'How could I overlook this?' Annika thought for a short while.

Annika went to the mirror as if in trance and put on her shoes. She looked great. Then she read the big sign. Twice, to be on the safe side. It said in red letters 'Special offer today only – Ladies shoes 4,000 Icelandic Crowns!'

It took a load off her mind and a healthy colour slowly returned back to her face. She now knew the price and that she had enough money.

'Thank you, you wicked witch,' she thought. She was confused but relieved. Now she could go and pay without needing to say anything.

She just had to wait for a moment until all the other customers had left. It was safer this way. She had just made a huge fool of herself and wanted to avoid any even more unpleasant comments.

Then she went to the till and put the shoes on the table.

'So, will you take these?'

She nodded.

Shortly after, Annika was back in the street with her new shoes. Now they were officially bought and duly paid for. She had done it without Ragnar's help. Tears welled up in her eyes.

'Perhaps in the future, I should somehow tell people what the problem is,' Annika pondered. That would protect her from any inconveniences and misunderstandings. Annika was now completely lost in thought. She was lucky things had not turned out worse but now something became clear to her.

'Perhaps I might need something to show,' she thought. 'A card that explains selective mutism with a short and simple text would be ideal.'

'And if I had to deal with certain people for longer, I should consider making it known beforehand. Surely other people would be much nicer to me then?'

Annika liked her helpful ideas. The world was not prepared for someone who got speechless sometimes.

But she could not help it.

43

The couple Margret and Oskar liked Seyðisfjörður very much. Even before they had reached the place, they both had been thrilled by the scenery. They saw the sea in the valley and the mountains all around the place. Now they were looking for the harbour. They had turned into a side road. But there was no harbour but a dead end.

'Wrong turn again,' Margret ranted.

'You can drive if you know better!' Oskar snapped back.

Margret was offended and kept quiet.

Annoyed, she looked out of the window. Suddenly, she saw a house with an eye-catching sign. It was hanging on the fence and it said, 'For Sale.'

'Oh, look,' Margret shouted excitedly, 'I could like that!'

'Haven't you always wanted a house in the mountains and at the sea? That would also be great if we wanted to holiday in peace.'

'I'd like to take a closer look at this,' Margret talked on.

Oskar said spontaneously, 'Well, let's go in.'

And so he stopped, and they looked at the house at close range.

The house was painted in green from the outside and had two storeys. It was made of wood and had wide windows. For both of them coming from the city, it seemed like a magical hut, but there was a heavy off-road vehicle parked in front of the door.

There was a small courtyard to be seen in the adjacent property. In there was a trampoline and a bicycle. Other toys were also visible.

'Look, children also live here,' Margret whispered.

When both were standing at the fence, the front door of the house suddenly opened.

A young lady in a business suit and carrying a briefcase in her hand stepped outside. She seemed visibly annoyed.

She saw Margret and Oskar and smiled at them as quickly as a flash.

Then she shouted, 'Hi there, hello. Would you like to view the house?'

Oskar replied, 'Yes, gladly.'

'Well, then come in, please.'

She stretched out her hand.

'Welcome. I'm the estate agent here. Please enter.'

'Thanks. It's lovely here,' Margret purred.

'Nice to meet you,' Oskar said.

They crossed the doorstep. Behind the front door was a bright room with a decorated fireplace. Margret looked in all corners. A magnificent chandelier hung from the ceiling. The walls were painted in white. They were perfect for antique paintings. Margret and Oskar had inherited a few of these from an uncle.

'I was just about to leave. I had a viewing planned for today. Unfortunately, my client didn't show up,' the estate agent explained.

'Oh, then you're lucky that we came along,' Oskar joked.

'What a coincidence!'

They laughed.

Then the estate agent's mobile phone rang.

'Excuse me, I need to answer this. Please feel free to look around here on your own.'

'With pleasure,' Oskar and Margret said at the same time.

Margret went to the left towards the kitchen. There was a modern cooker and all kinds of household appliances. She especially liked the blue tiles above the fridge.

Oskar had ended up in the living room.

'Oh, nice and big,' he thought. 'That's the perfect spot for the TV.'

The bedrooms were up the stairs.

'Cool,' Margret shouted.

Both saw a small fenced in garden from out of the window.

'Really, I like it here,' Margret jabbered away.

'Look, the old bed could go there,' she went on and on to Oskar.

'And the green sofa would fit in there.'

'Whatever you say.'

'Yes, of course. And there is space for the armchair. You know the one we ditched and put into the storeroom last year.'

Then the estate agent came around the corner.

'So, did you have a look around?' she asked.

'Yes. We find it very lovely here.'

'Great, this is our leaflet. If you want to fill this in, I can send you further information.'

'Thank you very much.'

'If you want to buy the house, I need to know by tomorrow. The quicker you sign the contract, the better. I also have other clients, you know.'

'By tomorrow?' Margret exclaimed, startled.

'Yes, unfortunately. The sellers have had it on the market for way too long and an important meeting is planned for tomorrow. You should definitely come along if you are interested in the house.'

'But we're on a mission,' Oskar said.

'Yes, we need to find a treasure,' Margret barged in.

'Oh, I'm sorry but if you can't be there tomorrow, we'll most probably sell the house to someone else.'

'That's a pity.'

'Yes, I'm so sorry.'

'Come on, let's think about it again.'

'Please let me know.'

All three left the house.

'I need to go now. Thank you. See you.'

The estate agent disappeared.

'You know what, let's just stay here,' Margret said and took a piece of chocolate out of her handbag.

'And forget about the treasure hunt?'

'Yes.'

'Don't you want the money anymore?'

'Oh, well, it's so beautiful here. And actually you've earned enough?'

'Yes, but it would be great to find the treasure?'

'Well, ... I ... actually I've had enough. The journey was stressful. Let's just stay here for a couple of days and relax, okay.'

'If you want it like that?'

'Yes, let's simply be spontaneous and enjoy the quiet.'

They laughed.

'That's how rural idyll can influence a city slicker,' Oskar said then.

'If you want to call it like that, honey,' Margret retorted with a satisfied smile.

So the couple finally decided to end their treasure hunt. They were happy to have found their dream house. They let the estate agent know that they wanted to take part in the meeting the next day. And that they wanted to buy the house. Then they got into their car and drove to the sea. They looked into the distance. The water hissed and the air smelled fresh.

And Oskar had revolutionary ideas once again.

'A bridge over the water, that would be the right thing,' he said.

'Exactly here.'

'Well, really, Oskar!' Margret sighed disgustedly.

'You can only think about work.'

'So, just let me do so,' Oskar bickered.

'Engineers always think.'

He squinted his eyes and shook his head briefly.

'If only there wasn't so much water.'

They laughed.

44

Ragnar and Annika were meanwhile on their way to the Dettifoss waterfall. They had bought cat food beforehand and provisions for themselves. The road was tarmacked and felt incredibly long. For a while, the route followed the banks of a winding river. Sometimes, there were individual houses. There was hardly any traffic. But they saw a police car that overtook them.

'Where are they going?' Annika asked.

Ragnar did not know either. Soon after, the traffic came to a halt.

'What's going on now?' Ragnar grumbled impatiently.

He got out. He walked along the road for a while, until he could see the beginning of the traffic jam.

There was the police car. The police officers had set up a kind of roadblock. They slowly checked the vehicles in turn. They seemed to be looking thoroughly into the interior of the cars. They also checked the luggage compartments.

'Whom or what are they looking for?' Ragnar thought with worry.

'Had a convict escaped or what?'

He smirked, as this was pretty unlikely in this area. Ragnar went back to his car and Annika immediately asked what was wrong. His assumptions frightened Annika. Her thoughts were racing.

'They aren't looking for Felix, are they?'

'I don't believe that they'd put up such a fuss just because of a cat.'

'Oh, let's hope so.'

She looked out of the window to distract herself.

Ragnar slowly drove on and the roadblock came closer and closer. Annika wrapped Felix in her jacket and hid him under her seat. They did not need to see the cat. The police officer came up to Ragnar. He opened the window.

'Good afternoon, police check. Just two people?'

'Yes, only the two of us.'

'Well, please open the luggage compartment.'

The police officer shone a light into the interior of the car and saw that nobody was hiding there. Ragnar opened the luggage compartment and again the police officer saw that there was nothing suspicious in there.

'What are you looking for?' Ragnar asked hesitantly.

'I'm sorry. I'm not allowed to tell you,' the police officer replied. 'Thank you. You can drive on. Er... Have a safe journey.'

'Thanks. Goodbye!'

Ragnar closed the luggage compartment again and drove on.

'Well, we made it through,' he said.

Annika had taken Felix in her arms.

'Good thing.'

She cuddled Felix and he purred.

Gunnar had also reached the tail end of the traffic jam and had settled in.

'Let's see how long this will take,' he thought.

When he reached the point where his vehicle was checked, he happened to overhear two police officers having a conversation. They seemed to just be on a break.

'We won't find the gal today. She's miles away for sure.'

'Well, too bad that you only know as an adult how wonderful it is at home. These runaways are only looking for a little bit of fun.'

'We were all young once. Hey, there's a customer, I'll be off then.'

He had seen Gunnar and the cargo area of his truck was scrutinised by several police officers very thoroughly.

'Nobody's hitched a ride with me,' Gunnar exclaimed.

'Fair enough, you can move on then. Have a nice day.'

Consequently, the unplanned stop for Gunnar had also been taken care of now.

Anton had been following the others all the time and found out that they wanted to go to Dettifoss. He got through the roadblock without problems and eagerly made plans how he could best harm the others and outplay them.

45

Annika and Ragnar eventually arrived at the waterfall. They parked at a distance from it. Then they walked on. Annika's new shoes were comfortable, and she was sure she would not get any blisters on her feet. Felix stayed back in the car.

Dettifoss was really very impressive. They both saw the giant waterfall. It was cold but it was worth being there for this great natural spectacle. And the noise of the water rushing down was even more impressive. Annika took a few photos that she wanted to show to her mother later. She would wonder where Annika had been.

You could directly walk to the edge of the waterfall. But where would someone hide a treasure or the next clue for it here? The ground was rocky. From time to time, water splashed onto the tourists on the path. Annika and Ragnar saw how the roaring water poured down there and frothed fiercely. It was terribly loud.

Anton had arrived at the waterfall shortly after and walked near to where Annika and Ragnar were still standing. Anton started looking for the treasure under rocks. While doing so, he disturbed other tourists who indignantly turned away. He eventually approached Ragnar and Annika.

He said provokingly,'You won't find anything, ha-ha.'

Ragnar replied calmly, 'We haven't found anything yet. We're still looking. We've already found so many clues; we'll also find this one soon. I'm sure!'

'You won't!' Anton scoffed. 'You're too stupid for that.'

'We won't let you tell us anything! We'll work it out for ourselves!'

'Nope, I'll handle this differently,' Anton retorted and threatened a punch with his fist.

'Please, let's behave properly,' Ragnar begged but he already felt Anton's breath very close. What followed was a dull pain and he shrieked.

There was a real fight between Anton and Ragnar. The two men held on to one another and Anton tried non-stop to hit Ragnar with punches. He was good at sidestepping but did get one or two hits. Meanwhile, Annika stood by, petrified, unable to do anything.

Suddenly, Gunnar was on the scene and helped Ragnar. After a short brawl, the two men brought Anton under control. He fidgeted and shouted out all possible insults, but nobody cared. Gunnar tried to hold his mouth shut but to no avail. Anton bit him in the finger and he had to let go.

'Darn,' Gunnar sighed. 'Stop it!'

'Let go of me!' Anton shouted in despair, while he tried to break free from his awkward position.

'You will regret that!'

46

Suddenly, the four of them heard a plane. The engine noise came closer. They saw a plane with a colourful banner in the air. Something was written on it. The wind was strong and so at first, they could not read what was on the fluttering banner.

'Anyone got binoculars?' Ragnar shouted excitedly to other tourists. But nobody had any ready to hand.

'I can see it now,' Anton shouted when he stared up straightaway. 'I ain't blind yet! It says Good Luck! ... Ha-ha-ha.'

The next moment, lots of colourful slips fell out of the plane.

'Someone is dropping something,' Ragnar realised as fast as lightning.

'Quick, try to catch a slip,' he instructed Annika.

Most of the slips fell directly into the water but Annika managed to catch one on the rocky ground. The next riddle was indeed on it.

Go, it's much at stake
To a volcanic mosquito lake
Mineral-rich water is healthy
This place makes you wealthy!

The plane disappeared again.

'It's getting funnier and funnier,' Ragnar said, baffled. 'Someone must have organised this, especially for us.'

'Yes, looks like it. Someone is watching us and our progress,' Annika whispered in Ragnar's ear, as Anton and others were in earshot and Annika's unwritten rules of selective mutism required it to be.

'NO ONE MUST HEAR!'

'Perhaps the ghost of Fridrik Jonsson?'

'No.'

'Or the lady from the hotel in Reykjavik? What was her name again?'

'Inga.'

'Yes, ... that's crazy,' Ragnar replied. 'And what are we going to do with him?' he went on and pointed to Anton. Gunnar was still holding the attacker tight.

But just at that moment, when Ragnar and Gunnar were distracted briefly, Anton was able to break free from their grip. He ran away, as fast as it was actually possible on this ground.

'The treasure hunt isn't over yet!' Anton shouted angrily.

'You'll see!'

Ragnar and Gunnar were shocked for a while but accepted then that Anton had escaped.

'What the hey,' Ragnar wheezed. 'And onward it goes! The lake is waiting for us tomorrow.'

47

Gunnar had immediately returned to his truck after the fight, where he wanted to spend the rest of day. He had arranged warm blankets and he just wanted to curl up when he heard something outside.

It was a woman. She was beautiful but she looked thin in her long coat, and she seemed to be in need of help. She knocked firmly on the driving cab.

''ello?' the woman shouted with a French accent.

Gunnar opened the door.

'Who's there? What's up?'

'I need 'elp, please.'

'What's the matter?'

'Can I 'itch a ride?'

'Where to?'

'No matter where, I go anywhere,' the woman said.

'But it's late already, I won't go anywhere else today,' Gunnar said apologetically.

'Please 'elp!'

The woman tread on the spot in despair. She was visibly shivering.

'Just come in, it's warm in my living room,' Gunnar joked eventually. 'And I have plenty of space.'

Gunnar allowed the woman to get in. She sat down in the vacant seat and muttered softly,

'Merci.' After a short pause, she continued.

'I mean... thank you.'

'You're welcome,' Gunnar said. 'By the way, I'm Gunnar. Here's something to eat and I also have coffee left,' he said offering her a biscuit.

'Oh, thank you. My name is Colette.'

'Pleased to meet you.'

'I come from France.'

Her long hair covered parts of her face, while she was speaking.

'Oh, that sounds interesting. And where are you heading?' Gunnar was suddenly very nonchalant. He thought that Colette was very nice.

'I want to see the world,' she replied. 'Iceland is exciting.'

'Yes, I quite believe that. Pretty brave of you, just on your own.'

'Oh, I like being abroad and got used to it.'

She ate and drank, and they both kept on chatting. Gunnar learnt that she had hitch-hiked this far, but her ride was not going any further. She had already been staying in Iceland for a while and just wanted to get to know the island. As she had no accommodation, he decided to allow her to stay in his truck. Gunnar also promised to give her a lift in the morning.

But before they could go on to the lake, they really needed to sleep for a few hours first.

48

Anton had kept watching Ragnar and Annika and followed them from the car park to their accommodation for the night. He sneaked up on it. After losing the fight at the waterfall, he had decided in revenge to slow them down.

How could he do that best?

It had been Anton who had crashed into Ragnar and Annika on the road days ago. He had felt powerful at the time, and he wanted to show this to them. He wanted to gain some respect. Surely you did not mess with him.

Now Anton felt incredibly angry.

These two always knew everything better and if he did not do anything, they would find the treasure and not he. Because of that, Anton had to develop a plan.

He needed to steal something, he suddenly thought. His sudden hunger gave him an idea. He had watched Ragnar had a box with food and drinks in the luggage compartment of his car. He had to get at their provisions. They had so much to eat, and he had nothing. This was just like it had been in the past. And his upsetting memories made him even angrier.

As a child, he had suffered very much from poverty. He knew what it meant to starve. Sometimes, the fridge at home had been empty for days. His mother was depressed most of the time and unable to look after him when she was drinking. And she did that often. His father had beaten him constantly. He worked day and night, and little Anton was glad then when he was not there because at least he did not get a beating then. One day, his father went away and did not come back. Later, Anton learnt that he was not alive anymore. He had never understood how this could have happened. His mother said that it was an accident. 'At least no more beating,' Anton thought at the time.

Anton quickly swept away this memory from his thoughts and got on with his task. The lock of Ragnar's car was quickly picked and he disappeared with the delicious stuff just as quickly.

Anton examined his loot with satisfaction. There was bread and cheese, apples, oranges and bananas. He ate hastily and it tasted great. His eyes were heavy. He yawned.

Then he went to bed. But he could not fall asleep. In his mind were thoughts upon thoughts.

'Hopefully, they won't starve to death.'

And suddenly, Anton felt guilty.

49

Annika and Ragnar quickly noticed the next day that somebody had broken into their car. But only their provisions were missing.

'Weird, was that a tramp?' Ragnar wondered in bewilderment. 'Who else would only be interested in the food?'

Annika was immediately frightened and annoyed again but she wanted to quickly continue on their journey anyway.

'I'm so hungry,' she griped.

'We'll buy some new stuff,' Ragnar reassured her with a short pat on her forearm.

'You're so nice!' she reciprocated the nice gesture.

'I'll do anything for you,' was Ragnar's telling reply.

He looked Annika directly in the eye and automatically thought they are beautiful eyes.

They laughed.

They drove on to the lake. Suddenly, it was raining heavily. It was only a shower of rain but no snow. At this moment, it was not cold enough for that. But Ragnar did not see very well because of the heavy rain drops on the windscreen. He was moving forward slowly and only hoped that they would arrive soon unharmed.

At the same time, Gunnar and Colette were on their way to the lake. The truck was prepared for the weather and suddenly Gunnar felt more alive in company. Colette was very talkative and the music from the radio helped them to perk up.

Anton had also been on his way to the said lake called Mývatn. As he had hardly slept, he felt like nothing on earth, but his anger was still there. He would certainly have another ace up his sleeve to get this treasure in the end because he believed success was due to come to him and nobody else.

50

Annika and Ragnar eventually reached the geothermal area that was next to the ring road and signalled the proximity of the lake. The land was a little snowed in, but the road was clear. To the left and right of the road, there were brown hills without vegetation. In some places, steam came out of the ground. Here, the fire from the interior of the earth in the shape of hot water and the ice of the wintry weather clashed in a fascinating manner. It stank of rotten eggs and Annika remembered how it had been near Strokkur days ago.

'Let's get out of here. I don't want to go there. Besides, the riddle sends us to the lake. If the treasure is finally there?'

'We only drive through this. We'll be at the lake soon,' replied Ragnar.

'Good. I'm curious how it'll be there. But shall I tell you something about the lake?'

'Go ahead. I'd like to know more.'

Annika had researched and found interesting information.

'I have read Mývatn is a volcanic lake in the northeast of Iceland. The name means Mosquito Lake. I wonder whether they have lots of mosquitoes there?' she said.

'Surely not in the cold. But in the summer perhaps.'

'Right and there are also lots of fish and birds there, even though the lake is relatively shallow.'

'How deep is it actually?'

'About four metres.'

'Can you swim in there?'

'Unfortunately, I haven't read anything about that. But there's a public bath somewhere here.'

'Well, I don't want to in this cold. Also not in hot springs or so. Besides, we don't have time.'

The landscape was recovering slowly again, and the pungent smell of sulphur was gone. They had come to a place where all sorts of accommodation were available.

'You can also drive around the lake. But that'd be almost 40 kilometres.'

'I believe we'll stay here at the main road for the moment.'

'But the main road only goes along in the north and in the west,' Annika knew because she was looking at the map. 'But the small airport is there. Can you see the runway in this direction?'

'Oh, interesting. But a few remote places here have their own airport! That's handy.'

They drove on and suddenly, they were driving on the lakeside so that they could catch a glimpse of the water now and again. It was wonderful how it lay in front of them.

'Is the lake frozen over in winter?' Ragnar asked.

'I don't think so, there are hot springs underneath.'

'Oh, interesting. And why are there mountains sticking up out of the lake?'

'These are pseudo craters, so no real volcanoes. They form when a hot lava stream gets together with water and there's a steam explosion,' Annika explained.

'You've prepared yourself really well,' Ragnar praised her with a smile. 'I didn't want to know that in detail.'

'Sure, what do you think?' She gave him a slight push against his arm.

Now both laughed.

'Where shall we start looking here?' Annika asked. 'The lake is huge!'

'We need something to eat. Tell me Annika, how about doing something really special today? I invite you out for a meal if you fancy that?'

'Sure. Certainly, there are really elegant restaurants here at this cool lake. It's also a holiday area, isn't it?'

'Right, let's see then.'

'Well, I'm excited.'

Ragnar and Annika seemed to be getting along increasingly well. With every day that they spent together, they knew each other better. They reached a junction where they could either continue to drive around the lake or away from the lake towards the west.

'What now?' Ragnar asked anxiously. 'Go back or ... oh, what the hey, we're going around the lake from the other side and going back to the place we started from. We can get out there, right? There's not much more here. I bet the treasure is in this place.'

'Agreed, let's do it like that.'

And so Ragnar turned left, and they spotted the water again after a short drive. They were at the south side of the lake now. They saw people on horses and Annika asked Ragnar.

'Can you ride a horse?'

'No, never tried.'

'Me neither. But that would be funny indeed. It's all moving, isn't it? If you're sitting on the back of a horse. And how does it start off? And how do you stop?'

'No idea. Perhaps you should take riding lessons.'

Annika smiled and looked dreamily at the clouds. They passed a big hotel and crossed over a river. Then the lake came back into view again. Snow-covered spots made the otherwise sparse landscape look like a cow pattern.

Annika looked out of the window, while the radio was playing music. She noticed lava formations that looked like small towers. Finally, they both came to a viewpoint with a car park that was directly next to the road. Ragnar stopped.

'I just need to stretch my legs,' he said. 'And you can take a look here whether there's a clue.'

'Well, it's so beautiful here. I'd like to stay here for longer.'

Ragnar got out. And he walked a bit up and down. Annika also got out in order to take photos. The lake reached into the distance. She could hear the whooshing of the water. Were there waves as well? But otherwise, there was nothing.

Then they drove on to another car park where again there was no sign of a clue. Bare-branched bushes and snow were at the roadside. In the distance, there were craters to be seen. Then the road proceeded away from the lake again and they could not see the water anymore. They saw several buildings. There was a sign in the shape of a cow with a black-and-white colour pattern. And the sign said Farm Cafe. Annika loved the sign.

'Do we want to take a look here and see what they have to eat? Or drink a coffee?' Ragnar suggested.

Annika nodded. 'And go to the toilet.'

'Exactly,' Ragnar retorted and pressed his legs together.

They turned off the road and there was another sign at the entrance. 'We have great pizza', it said in English.

'That's convenient,' Annika thought. 'I could eat a horse now.'

51

There was a large car park in a giant courtyard. Alongside, there was a meadow and the water. They got out but Felix had to stay in the car on his own.

'I'm just looking outside quickly, okay. Just do go ahead and choose something. I'll be there in a minute,' Annika said.

'Sure, will do. Do you want pizza?'

'I'll have to look at the menu first.'

'Right, see you then.'

Annika went for a walk in the direction of the meadow. She saw four brown and two black cows that were grazing peacefully. The lake was calm, and the water felt cool. Annika had put her hand into it. A treasure, a clue or a new riddle were also nowhere to be found here.

Then Annika went back to the café which was actually a farm, there were stables and different buildings. Suddenly, she saw a female child that had appeared and was coming closer. Annika wanted to run away but she thought it was too late. Because the child was already addressing her.

'Hello!'

'Lovely here, isn't it?'

Annika looked bewildered. But as nobody was there, she could say something quietly.

'What's your name?'

'Katrin. Do you have something to eat?'

'Hopefully, they'll have something in there.'

Katrin was perhaps 12 years old. Annika went to the car with her because she wanted to check on Felix. The cat was still there. He was sitting in the back seat and looked at Katrin with big eyes.

'Meow, meow,' Katrin exclaimed,

and she waved to Felix.

'Is this your cat?'

'Yes.'

Katrin showed the ring that she was wearing on her finger to the cat. Felix remained in his seat, unimpressed.

'Come, I'm going in there now to eat. Come with me. We'll also get you something.'

Annika walked in the direction of the house and Katrin followed her.

She opened the door and looked around. The eatery had a few patrons. At the window on one side, two police officers wearing their uniforms were sitting eating cake. A woman with a toddler was sitting next to them and at the adjacent table; there was an elderly man with a leg in a cast. She could not recognise Ragnar immediately.

But Ragnar was actually sitting at a table in the corner. He had taken off his hat and he was waving. And so Annika and Katrin could join him.

'Who's this, Annika?' he asked with surprise.

But before she could answer, Katrin said loudly,

'Hello, I'm Katrin. We've met outside. I like her cat.'

'Hello Katrin. I'm Ragnar. Nice to meet you. ... Oh, Felix, you already know him?'

'Yes, of course. Felix, a wonderful name. And you are...?' She looked in Annika's direction.

Annika hesitated. Ragnar understood and helped her out.

'That's Annika. ... Er, ... Annika, what would you like to eat?'

The menu was lying on the table. Annika thumbed through it nervously. Katrin had also taken one and read.

'Are you hungry?' Ragnar asked.

'Yes, of course,' Katrin said.

'Then choose something, okay?'

There was indeed pizza on the menu. But there was also coffee and cake, tea, juice and all kinds of other stuff.

'Ham pizza!' Katrin exclaimed then.

'Okay, I'll take the one with mushrooms,' Ragnar said. 'And you Annika?'

Annika looked frightened. In this restaurant among other people, she could not order for herself. After all, the rule was: 'NO ONE MUST HEAR!'

She turned the menu towards Ragnar and pointed to ham pizza with spinach.

'Okay, I'll order then.'

'So what do you want to drink?' Ragnar asked when a server was close by.

'I'll take a coffee. Okay Annika, tea. And Katrin?'

She took a juice. Ragnar still knew what Annika had usually wanted the other days.

When that was done, Ragnar asked Katrin, why she was there on her own.

'We're here on holiday,' the girl claimed.

'We? ... Where are your parents?' Ragnar asked.

'They'll come later. They wanted to go shopping.'

'Without you?'

'I didn't want to go with them.'

'Do you like it here at the lake?' Ragnar kept on asking.

'Yes, it's great.'

She giggled.

Later on, food and drinks were on the table. They did not talk, just ate. Katrin had gone to the toilet and so Ragnar and Annika were alone at the table for a moment.

Suddenly, Ragnar turned around and could not believe his eyes. He looked to Annika.

'Isn't that the ...what was his name again?'

'Where?'

The one sitting over there. He discretely pointed.

'Oh, my goodness, yes! He looks like him,' Annika whispered quietly.

'Ask him for an autograph. Quick. Please,' she begged.

They saw a well-known singer at another table reading the paper. Ragnar went to get his autograph which he supplied without question. Ragnar then wanted to go to the toilet and in the corridor there, he saw a notice on the wall. The big headline on it was, Missing. Now he looked closer. There was a photo of Katrin! He got a fright. He went back to the table quickly, to Annika.

'Do you know what, Katrin is wanted. There's a notice! ... And police officers are sitting over there.'

'Oh dear, I'm scared. What has she done? ... But you did get the autograph?'

'Why yes, that's no problem. But he's busy. He didn't want to talk for long.'

'Sure. Oh, she's coming back!'

Katrin adjusted her chair and sat down at the table again.

'What's up?' she asked. 'Why are you acting so strange?'

Ragnar needed to say something.

'Katrin...are you sure that your parents are here?'

She blushed.

'Er...well ...,' she stammered. Ragnar tried to help her.

'Your parents will really be worried if you just disappear like that. Come on, you should go home.'

'No! What do you know. All adults are the same. I'll never go back!'

'Think about it, you need food and accommodation. It's cold. What's so bad at home?'

'Nothing.'

'Come on, tell me. Trouble at school?'

'No. ... Er, yes. I'll fail at maths. And the teachers give me a hard time. And I also don't have any friends. And there's a boy, he's bullying me.'

'I see. And do your parents know?'

'Nope.'

'Well, they'll surely find a solution. If you tell this to your parents and also to your teachers at school, they will help you.'

'Well, I don't know.'

'Sure, very certainly. So... do you want to go back home now?'

'Ach... If it has to be.'

'There, the friendly police officers over there will surely take you back to your parents again, right? And then everything will be fine. You're so brave.'

'Very well. I'll try again at home and at school.'

She stood up.

Ragnar had let the police officers know in the meantime. They were very surprised but also glad that they would get the praise for finding the missing girl.

'Take care,' he said before Katrin went to the police officers.

'You, too. Bye Annika and also tell Felix bye from me!'

Ragnar and Annika waved to Katrin.

52

Annika and Ragnar continued their journey. They needed to cross a cattle grid and then, they were back again in the place where they had arrived at first. Unfortunately, they had not remembered the name of the place.

'We should have taken this route to begin with,' Ragnar said. 'Somehow, there was more to be seen.'

'Oh well, it was good to just see all that,' Annika replied. 'Such a beautiful scenery.'

They had circled the lake once completely and were still looking for the treasure or the next clue. Felix had hidden in the backseat during the journey and seemed to sleep. They went to the tourist information office of the said place. There, you could buy all sorts of gifts and picture postcards but there was no clue to a treasure. In the supermarket, they bought fresh food and drink for the journey ahead. Ragnar also wanted to go to the petrol station again, not that they would be forced to stop. But where was this treasure?

Anton had also arrived at the lake. He had lost sight of Ragnar and Annika for a short while, but he found them again here. He watched their shopping spree and asked himself what they would do next.

Gunnar had also arrived with Colette at Lake Mývatn in the meantime. They both had gone for a short walk. Before that, they had stopped at the geothermal area and looked at the lakes and taken photos of the steaming springs. They were hoping to discover a clue to finding the treasure somewhere here. But there was nothing and it got too cold for Colette. When they were back at their vehicle, Gunnar's phone was ringing.

Annika's phone was suddenly vibrating as well. She had set it on mute in the restaurant so that it would not ring in front of people because she experienced this attention as embarrassing. Ragnar's phone was ringing at the same time. Strange, they both thought but they pulled their devices out of their pockets and were astonished. There was a message from a number unknown to them.

It said 'Listen to Radio Mývatn! Now!'

Ragnar turned on the car radio immediately. Music was playing.

'We'll be waiting,' he said.

Then there was an announcement.

'An anonymous listener has sent us this wonderful poem; it's a lovely greeting to someone who hopefully knows what he or she has to do with it.'

The presenter read it out.

> *Now visit a lovely town*
> *Famous for its fish industry and a crown*
> *Take the westbound road even in snow and ice*
> *Then, you will find your great prize!*

'Well, if this isn't an invitation for a trip, what else? Surely, your prize will be waiting there! Ha-ha. ...And now, music again, here at Radio Mývatn.'

'That was meant for us!' Ragnar exclaimed.

'We're supposed to go further westward. Wait, I'll look it up. There's a town, Akureyri. And there's fish industry there.'

'I'm gobsmacked, on the radio! Whoever controls this treasure hunt must really carry weight, right? Can that actually be Inga?'

'Definitely. Think of the plane!'

'True.'

'Anyway, we just need somewhere to spend the night. I'm so tired.'

The other treasure hunters had also received a message and quickly turned on the radio. They were all baffled how this message had got there at the right time.

Gunnar had been walking with Colette for a while. The exercise was good for him.

'Tell me, is it actually the polar circle 'ere?' she suddenly asked.

'Yes, we're a little below it, I believe,' Gunnar explained patiently.

'That's why it's only light for a few 'ours 'ere?'

'Yes but it isn't polar night here yet. Then the sun wouldn't come up at all. Like at the North Pole. Well, I don't really know for sure.'

'I 'ave 'eard that it must be beautiful in the summer, the midnight sun?'

'Oh yes, you must see that. But the white nights are just the compensation for the darkness now,' Gunnar confirmed.

They both looked at the sky. This time, they had also taken rooms in a remote hotel. They saw the northern lights before they fell asleep.

53

Annika and Ragnar were sleeping in a guesthouse near the lake. It bordered on a field and was quiet during the night.

When Annika woke up, Felix was gone.

'Felix?' she cried. 'Where are you? Felix!'

The tomcat was gone. Panic rose in Annika.

'That can't be true.'

'Felix!' Nothing. She looked out of the window but could not recognise anything, as it was still dark. It was closed in any case. And the door was also closed.

'How did he get out?' she thought.

She dressed quickly. She had to go and search for the cat. In a hurry, she slipped into her trousers and put on her jacket. Quickly put her hat on and the scarf around her neck and then she was standing in front of her mirror and thought that she looked neat.

As she went to open the door, she realised that there was a kind of cat flap built in.

'Oh, I didn't see that yesterday,' she thought. 'Or was that an opening for mail or washing?'

It did not matter. The cat must have got out this way.

But where was he now?

She opened the door quietly. There was nothing to see. She walked a few steps, very carefully to not wake anyone up. It was very early in the morning. Suddenly, she heard a quiet whining. It came from a corner. She sneaked over there and bent down. There was Felix but his paw was stuck in a mouse trap. The iron frame had cut into his fur. That must have hurt. Felix was lying there without moving, but he had perked up his ears, as he reacted to Annika's arrival with a pitiful meow.

'Oh, there you are! I was worried sick about you,' Annika cried and jumped up and down with joy. She freed Felix from his predicament. He caterwauled shortly when she released his paw. But then, he had not really injured himself badly because he ran around without a limp. Apparently, he must have been lucky.

'Who sets up such a cruel thing,' she thought.

Just as she wanted to touch Felix and lift him again, she saw something else.

'Ahh!' she screamed.

The cat had given her a very special gift.

He had a mouse in his mouth. He now laid it down carefully on the carpet in front of Annika. She trembled.

'Oh, help, a mouse. Is it dead?'

Ragnar had heard the scream and had come running out of his room.

'What's going on...?'

He did not get any further because now he saw the mouse as well and an innocent looking cat that must have been asking himself what he had done wrong.

Annika was standing nearby, deathly pale.

'Everything okay?' he asked caringly. 'That's only a dead mouse. Cats do such things. They proudly show their prey to their mistress and want to play.'

He stepped aside a bit and petted Felix.

'You've really been successful on the hunt today, Felix,' he said with praise.

Then he turned around to Annika and said, 'Let the mouse lie there. We'll pack our stuff and drive on.'

Meanwhile, Felix considered the mouse as his breakfast.

54

Once again the weather was bad. This time it was slightly snowing when they came to the more mountainous parts. The sky was grey, and it had been quite dark all the time. They had left Mývatn behind and were driving further and further westward.

'I hope it won't get worse,' Ragnar said.

But it was getting misty, and it was snowing more heavily. Suddenly, there was a tremendous snowstorm. The wind was blowing strongly, and the snow was banging into the car windows. Ragnar drove to the side and stopped. He just wanted to take a short breather and await the worst. Later he realised that this had been a mistake because his vehicle got even more covered by drifting snow this way and it ended up partially snowed in.

He did not get any further. Ragnar and Annika were stuck in the snow. The tyres were spinning but the car would not move forwards or backwards. Very slippery spots had developed under the wheels due to his many attempts to get free.

'No way,' Ragnar exclaimed.

Annika looked around helplessly.

'What are we going to do now?'

'I think the weather is getting better. We'll wait and see. I've also got a shovel!'

'Someone is approaching!' Annika suddenly exclaimed.

'Is that Gunnar's truck?'

Gunnar stopped.

'Hey, can I help you?'

'Yes, please. As you can see, we're stuck.'

'Well, let me see then. I always have sand and a shovel with me. You do need to have these here, don't you?'

'Of course. Me too,' Ragnar said. 'A shovel, unfortunately no sand. But we'll handle that together.'

Ragnar and Gunnar grabbed a shovel each and alternately threw sand in front of Ragnar's tyres. Then he tried to break free again. It did not work.

Gunnar offered to push-start the car. Colette and Annika were also supposed to join in. Ragnar was accelerating gently. But that did not help either. Gunnar reckoned, they needed a starting aid. He remembered his equipment.

'I also have snow chains. But they aren't new and probably not in your size. They might totter a little, but it'll be fine. I really don't want to damage your car. Do you want to try these?'

As an experienced truck driver, Gunnar knew exactly what he was doing. And so he put the chains on professionally. They fitted relatively well; perhaps they were a bit loose. But they were certainly useful because they spanned an iron net around the tyre. These edges together with the loose parts of the chain links ensured that there was more grip on the ground and also prevented snow from getting stuck on the tyre. You have to drive more slowly on a public road with snow chains, but they were not supposed to stay on, once the car was freed.

Ragnar tried again.

They brought the car back into position again and Ragnar could drive on, as the snowstorm was over again as fast as it had come.

Gunnar took his snow chains back with him. Both he and Colette were happy that they were able to help to free the car.

'That could have been worse,' Gunnar said thoughtfully.

'Thank you for your help.'

'You're welcome. We were there just at the right time.'

They laughed.

'Hey, why don't we drive together?' Ragnar asked and smiled at Gunnar.

'My truck will just hold you back. This way you're faster,' Gunnar said. 'Besides, I'd like to be alone with Colette.' He smiled sheepishly. 'And we both want to enjoy the scenery. Perhaps, we'll even make a short detour if something interesting should come along our way by chance.'

He remembered that he was supposed to move more. With Colette, he liked his wanderings.

'If you think so. I'll see you later then.'

'Okay. See you later.'

They all drove on to Akureyri to find the hidden treasure there.

55

The welcome sign of Akureyri was impossible to overlook. Probably every place in Iceland has such a sign standing at the roadside to show where the place officially begins. Annika had collected important, general information about the town again.

'Akureyri is a town that's surrounded by mountains. It's basically the capital of north Iceland. Water winds along next to the place. It's situated at a fjord.'

'There's church there,' Ragnar interrupted.

'Yes and there's a botanic garden and an art museum as well.'

'Great, I like it here.'

'Yes and you'll also like the motorcycle museum and the aviation museum.'

'Oh, yes!'

'But we're looking for a treasure.'

'Yes but first we'll need to go shopping.'

'Well. Of course, there are also supermarkets here. '

When they arrived at the town centre of Akureyri, they bought a small cage and toys for the cat as well as cat food and fresh food for themselves, so that Felix could not run away again and they were all well provided for. But they could not find a vet and so a conclusive examination of Felix's paw would have to wait until they were back at home again.

Later they drove around the town and passed houses of all colours. They were massive and the red, green, blue or yellow of the outer walls shone out at them from a distance. In winter it got very cold here, with lots of snow and the inhabitants were well prepared.

Boat trips for whale watching got cancelled because of the bad weather; that is what it said on a sign near the tourist information. Accordingly, there was not much going on at the terminal. An iron chain blocked the way. There were usually several tours daily and if you were unlucky and saw no animals for once, there was usually the possibility to go out again with a different tour.

'I reckon you can also watch whales in Husavik at the other fjord,' Ragnar said.

'Sure, but that's more a bay. And it's not near the ring road and very far in the north,' Annika replied. 'And there's a whale museum there.'

'Sounds good but that's for another time.'

'First of all, we need to find something here.'

Ragnar and Annika were slightly tired from the long car journey. They decided to make arrangements for the night, as there were also a few hotels and holiday homes in this town. They quickly found accommodation and left their luggage there.

They looked at everything there and had discovered a barbecue.

But where in this town should they look for a treasure?

'Fish industry,' Ragnar pondered. 'Let's go to the harbour later then.'

'Tomorrow morning! Or we won't see anything.'

'Right or later today. We've got lights. First, I'd like to take a shower and rest a bit.' Ragnar grabbed a towel.

'We'll see. I'll take a closer look at the map.' Annika disappeared behind a squeaky door.

56

Anton knew his way around Akureyri very well because he used to work here as the person responsible for the urban greenspaces. He had heard the riddle on the radio and had immediately thought of the harbour when he had learnt about the fish industry and a crown. He knew that the cruise ship Crown Princess had been anchored in the town before. So he went directly to the harbour. And he found the next riddle first by chance. Unfortunately, it was not the treasure again and the treasure hunt was therefore not yet over.

On the wall of a fish factory, there was a giant, colourful picture that spanned the entire building. You could not overlook it, but you could only see it if you looked closely. It seemed to be sprayed on like graffiti and was a kind of caricature of how the fish was processed. Really colourful. The wall was subdivided into small rectangles and in each one, there was a picture. It began with the catching of the fish in the sea and then you could see how the fish got transported on an assembly line in a factory. Workers dismantled the fish and bones were removed. Further processing and packaging followed then. And right down at the bottom, there was another riddle.

Come to the ancient parliament valley
The best location for a rally
Geologically active, beautiful scenery
A national park, as it should be!

'I can't believe this,' Anton thought with delight. 'I've found it! Ha-ha-ha.'

He went closer and read it again. And at first he thought he had won now. Shortly after, he realised that he still needed to go on.

'Oh, no treasure again! How many riddles to go?' he thought unhappily.

Anton got back in his car and drove around the town with a heavy heart. Nonetheless, he still kept his eyes peeled. Thus, he saw by chance where Ragnar and Annika had settled. This offered him the opportunity to do something to delay them. He already had a brilliant idea.

57

Gunnar and Colette wanted to stroll through the town in Akureyri and rest afterwards. This also accorded with Gunnar's ambitions for more exercise. Going for a walk was actually also exercise.

They spent the night in a cheap hotel in the town. They both wanted to be together and were glad that they had got the last vacant room there. They ate fresh fish and were both happy that they had found each other. But they were too tired for further evening activities, they just wanted to sleep properly.

Gunnar already wanted to finish this tiring treasure hunt but Colette was having fun with it and encouraging him to continue.

'How many clues have there been and still no treasure? I don't believe in it anymore,' he had said. 'I'd rather be together with you and holiday at the water.'

'Oh please, I will 'elp! I've never found a treasure before,' she whined like a toddler jumping on one leg.

'As you wish. Let's go on searching.'

Gunnar made himself comfortable on the sofa. Colette could have the bed, he did not mind. It was too small and too uncomfortable for two. Sleeping in the same bed was simply not good. Both had realised this so often in their lives before. You got in the way of the other one's arms and legs. Each turn was felt by the other person, and you did not get a wink of sleep, only to get up feeling knocked out the next morning. Separately was the best solution for this hotel room. And to keep fit for the treasure hunt, they both had to be really well-rested.

Gunnar adjusted his pillow.

'But not before tomorrow. Or the day after tomorrow? I like this town. Wouldn't you like to stay for longer and see more of it?'

'Everything you want to show me.'

'Very well, I'll think of something then. Good night, Colette.'

'Sleep well, Gunnar.'

She blew him a kiss.

'Night!' he exclaimed smiling before the door shut.

Then Colette disappeared into the bathroom with her toothbrush in her hand, where she stayed for a long time. The shape of the lamp above the sink reminded her of something she could not suppress.

She stared into the mirror and asked herself how her sister in France was. Since a quarrel at Christmas five years ago, they had not seen each other again. When she came back from Iceland, she resolved to visit her immediately. At least, she believed that she had a boyfriend to introduce to her sister. Perhaps even a husband and soon also children. Her sister had already had all that for a long time. She also wanted to tell her about her travels and show her photos. She missed French food and simply her sister, the only relative that she still had since the death of her parents.

Colette was so tired that she felt her head heavy. She was pale. She brushed her teeth and switched off the lights. While doing so, she forgot her thoughts again. She then sneaked to bed quietly and was startled when there was a creak.

But Gunnar did not notice, as he had already fallen asleep.

58

Ragnar and Annika did eventually decide to drive to the harbour on the same day.

'Fish industry? But what does this have to do with a crown? Perhaps there's a brand of tinned fish with a crown as a logo on the tins?'

'Not that I remember. But where else are industrial areas here? It must be the harbour.'

'Perhaps it's hidden on a boat?'

Annika had interesting ideas. Felix could also be enthusiastic about fish; that is why it would be better if he did not get out of the car near the fish factories. He could have stayed at the accommodation, but he was lying asleep in the backseat once again and they let him lie there undisturbed. So far, Felix had not shown much interest in the new cage. He simply did not want to get in. And when he was inside and you closed the door, he meowed so miserably that Annika was not able to leave him alone in there.

'He is just not a cage animal.'

These had been Ragnar's words. So he should only be put in there if it was really necessary. After all, he was free when they had found him.

They eventually reached the harbour. They drove around and Annika looked in all nooks and crannies. She did not see any ships except for smaller boats. The treasure could not be there, could it? When Ragnar had to stop at a red light, a side road attracted Annika's attention.

'We'll go there now, Ragnar,' she said decisively.

No sooner said than done. And after a while, they reached the fish factory that Anton had already found before. And the colourful picture on the wall caught their eye and they read the next riddle.

'So it's Thingvellir!'

'Yes. But tomorrow!'

'Tonight we still have something else on. Something very special. Are you hungry, Annika?'

'Oh, yes. I'm curious what you're up to.'

They laughed.

Annika and Ragnar decided to have a barbecue before they went to bed. Why should something that was in their accommodation remain unused?

They had no idea that they were being watched by Anton.

59

Barbecue in the late evening sounded really great. This way they both could finally be alone in a relaxed atmosphere and enjoy their time together. As they had already discovered before, a small barbecue was available at the accommodation. They had considered whether meat or vegetables should be served. And then they had decided on fish. Fresh herring that they had just bought. There should also be enough for Felix.

The accommodation really offered a lot. A fire was started in the garden fireplace. Otherwise, it would have been too cold to sit outside for long. Annika thought this showed how practical Ragnar was.

Annika was sitting close to Ragnar who had taken off his golden hat. She warmed herself by the fire. The flames were bright and there were slight sizzling noises.

'Tell me, this police block recently, was that because of Katrin?'

'Katrin?'

'The runaway girl from the lake.'

'Oh, yes. Could be. I think you're right.'

'Hopefully, she's at home now and safe.'

'I would think so. You can rely on the police.'

They laughed.

Ragnar put the food on the grill. It smelled delicious. Annika could see how the fish was cooking. Ragnar carefully tended to the barbecue and occasionally turned the fish around. It was supposed to get nicely brown and crispy on all sides.

When it was ready, they ate the fish. It was seasoned very well. That was also thanks to Ragnar. He had secured himself an appropriate blend of spices.

Felix licked his paws. He meowed. Then he fell asleep next to his new cage.

'He's cute, Ragnar, isn't he?'

'Yes, he knows what he wants.'

Ragnar also knew what he wanted, that is to say Annika. But he did not want to scare her. She would certainly like it to take it slowly. Ragnar cleaned everything up after the meal and they sat together outside for a while. The sky was dark.

'Do you like the stars?' Annika asked.

'Yes, when I can recognise a constellation, then I find that beautiful.'

'Oh, you're too scientific.'

'Ha-ha.'

'Look, it's green now.'

Annika and Ragnar suddenly realised that it was the northern lights. They were pale but visible.

'What a beautiful green,' Annika said. 'Totally cool.'

'And it is something romantic,' Ragnar reckoned and added: 'I also have an appreciation of beautiful things.'

He stroked her cheek. She cringed, as if it was unpleasant to her.

'You've had a hair there,' Ragnar said bashfully.

'Okay, thanks.'

'You have lovely delicate skin and the most gorgeous blue eyes.'

Ragnar gently stroked Annika's arm. She tolerated it. But Ragnar wanted more. They soon held hands. That was pleasant for Annika.

When they stood up from their chairs, they were still holding hands.

'I will be with you forever,' Ragnar said and began dancing gently on the spot. She did not resist.

How should he tell her? How would she react? He simply had to try directly. The moment seemed suitable. Tentatively, he started,

'I'd like to tell you something, Annika.' He stalled for a short while but then went on talking.

'I love you.'

She stared at him and smiled.

'I love you, too.'

She had returned his feelings without hesitation. He had known it. She also wanted him. He had perceived her smitten looks for days already.

A kiss was in the air. They gazed into each other's eyes.

'Now you look like a princess... No, a queen.'

'What?'

Annika had not expected Ragnar's tender advances that quickly. But she liked the compliments. The appropriate response was still difficult for her.

Ragnar did not care. He was in love and found more equally flattering words.

'My Queen Annika!'

60

Anton had nasty plans.

In the night, when everyone was sleeping, he sneaked up to Ragnar's car without a sound. He had to be careful not to be seen by anyone. The place was unlit, and a few bushes gave him protection.

But it was a problem when dogs barked, when he was doing something forbidden. He had already thought of having sausages with him in case there were guard dogs that needed to be distracted. But he was lucky, there were no dogs.

He kneeled down to the left front tyre and struck into it, deliberately puncturing the rubber. He quickly went on to the next tyre and did the same and so on until he had punctured all four of them. He had used extra-long and pointy nails for this that made only small penetrations so that his deed would stay unnoticed for as long as possible. These nails were like thin needles. 'Often there were nails lying about on the road,' Anton thought. No one would suspect this had been deliberate.

The tyres were not yet visibly flat. The holes were tiny and a small nail was stuck in each one. Surely, the escape of the air would take a while. A so-called slow puncture. No, even four!

Anton was satisfied with himself at this moment.

Because he knew, Annika and Ragnar would probably not get very far.

61

Annika and Ragnar immediately wanted to drive on to Thingvellir the next day. They had got up in high spirits after their romantic evening. Ragnar was humming a little song to himself, and Annika had tried out a strong perfume. She smelled of lovely violets and roses.

'Hopefully that wasn't too much,' she thought. She did not usually use perfume, but she had found it in the bathroom.
'I hope he'll be pleased,' Annika worried. 'And what if he doesn't like it?'

But Ragnar said nothing at all until they were sitting in the car, when he suddenly said,

'I like your new perfume.'

So he had noticed it. She was so happy.

Then Ragnar kissed Annika on both cheeks.

Being in love felt so wonderful, she wished that it would never end. She had the impression that he felt the same.

They got into the car without looking at the tyres. They drove off and Ragnar suddenly noticed that something was not right with the steering mechanism. Did it feel strange or was he just dreaming? The car had just been in the workshop before the treasure hunt started to have the brakes checked and everything else had been alright.

Then he suddenly realised that something was not right with the tyres. Because a display on the car dashboard lit up. This light blatantly screamed that the pressure in the tyres was not right.

'Weird, low tyre pressure,' he thought. 'I certainly didn't drive over a kerbstone or is it because we used the snow chains yesterday? Whatever, air is needed now.'

Ragnar stopped at the next opportunity, got out, walked around the car and checked the tyres. He was baffled. He understood the problem immediately. The tyres were flat. All four! He could see very clearly that there was no air inside anymore. And now Ragnar remembered that there had been such a strange clacking noise there all the time and he had ignored it. He had actually turned the radio off and had listened but it did not seem to be anything serious, so he had turned the radio back on again.

With a heavy heart, he informed Annika about the problem.

'Oh dear!'

'What shall we do?'

'That's impossible? All four of them at the same time?'

'I can't believe it.'

'There can't really be so many nails on the road all at once. Someone did that on purpose!'

'Vandalism in this lonely wilderness!'

'We need to call for help.'

'I've forgotten to charge my phone. It's switched off now. No power. I'm sorry.'

'Oh, I'm sorry, mine is flat, too. Our barbecue was simply too good. I forgot everything after that.'

'Oh ... remind me of that, now that everything is over.'

Annika had tears in her eyes.

'It'll be fine.'

'How? Well, Gunnar probably won't help us this time, will he? Where is he anyway?'

'I have no idea.'

'Ha-ha!'

Suddenly, Anton joined them. He was very nonchalant, and he was chewing chewing gum. He was sarcastic as always when he saw the flat tyres.

'Did we drive over a nail?'

'Oh, actually four! Ha-ha.'

Ragnar did not react. But he looked grim.

Anton offered him a chewing gum.

'Peppermint flavour. You'll feel better then!'

Ragnar thanked him and put it in his mouth immediately. The scent was pleasant in his nose. The chewing relaxed him, and he liked the fresh flavour.

Then Anton handed a chewing gum to Annika.

Annika declined shaking her head. She did not like peppermint flavour.

'Oh well, ... does the cute, tiny mute lamb not like chewing gum? I'll show you with pleasure what I'd want to chew with you. You'll scream then!'

Annika got frightened and froze. She was very certainly not a cute, tiny mute lamb. Why was everyone always so mean to her?

Anton had been invasive and had made a cheeky pass but did not really help with their breakdown. He took a step backwards; anticipating Ragnar's anger soon hit him. He was right.

He had gone too far for Ragnar who reacted impulsively.

'Get out of here or I'll think it over again what I'll do with you!' Ragnar called after him.

Anton sneered at him and giggled menacingly but turned away. He had parked his car out of view.

'Could he not have helped us?' Annika asked when he was gone. 'Perhaps he could have called someone or got help somewhere?'

'I don't trust him. He might set us up to be robbed by his cronies. He's capable of anything.'

'Anyway, he was our only chance. If nobody else comes past.'

62

Anton was now in the lead. Uncatchable. Nobody would be able to provide evidence for his deeds. He drove as fast as he could to Thingvellir to get his treasure. The thought of it spurred him even more. With tunnel vision, he stared at the road in front of him. The road conditions were good, allowing him to increase his lead without any problems.

No matter how many riddles were left to solve, he would find them first and eventually also the treasure at the end. It was time that he took this seriously and became more than just a bystander.

He had eliminated his keenest competition with Ragnar and Annika. He did not really consider Gunnar with his slow truck as a worthy opponent and if anyone else was still in the race, they would not be able to seriously compete with him as they would be too far behind. He had not seen anyone else for quite some time.

The end of his money troubles was within reach. He imagined digging out a chest full of gold. He saw himself being treated like a king. He would pamper attractive young women and he could afford the poshest car in the neighbourhood.

He was so lost in his thoughts; he did not see a pothole. It was really there, and it gave him such a jolt that went through his entire body because he was driving so fast.

Luckily, his car did not get damaged.

'I need to be careful,' he thought. 'It's all or nothing.'

He would be the winner of this treasure hunt.

63

'We'll handle it. Don't worry,' Ragnar said because he saw Annika's look of panic. Her eyes were big, and she was breathing fast. Tears ran down her cheeks. She trembled intensely. Her hair was completely tousled.

'Where are Gunnar and Colette?' Annika asked again.

'As I said, no idea.'

'Did they leave before us or after us? What do you think?'

'How should I know? They didn't want to come with us!'

Suddenly, Ragnar felt hot.

'Is it warmer now?' he asked with bewilderment.

'No, I'm freezing,' Annika retorted.

Ragnar suddenly did nothing and stared into space. Nobody came past who could help. Despair was writ large on their faces.

'We've come this far!' Ragnar said.

'But it isn't going on, unfortunately.'

The two of them were very sure that this was the end of their adventure.

'We won't get these fixed that quickly.'

'And all four of them,' Ragnar moaned.

'Yes.'

'There is nobody and nothing here. And surely nobody will come.'

'Yes.' Annika said and she opened her bag. 'And it's so cold here. I'll put on some more clothes!'

'We could have died!' Ragnar continued, horror-stricken. 'If a tyre suddenly bursts... I don't want to think about that.'

Annika was paler than ever before. But Ragnar got more and more agitated.

'Anton will in any case be there before us now,' he screamed.

'Exactly. Unfortunately,' Annika mumbled softly.

'And we can't go on,' he ranted. He flailed his arms about wildly. Annika got frightened but only gave a super short answer.

'Yes.'

'We'll need to give up. I'm so sorry.'

'Yes. Me too.'

That must have been the blackest day in Ragnar and Annika's life. There was no hope anymore.

The treasure hunt was definitely over for the two of them now.

64

Ragnar wanted to give free rein to his tears and at the same time hit a sandbag. Unfortunately, he did not have one at the moment.

So it was really over.

He could not stoop any lower. He pushed his golden hat almost into his eyes.

Suddenly, he felt dizzy. That had to be the shock. Everything was spinning but he did not let it show. He saw his car double and at the next moment completely blurred. Then everything was normal again. He blinked.

He suddenly felt full of energy and his heart beat faster. His forehead was shining but his hands were cold.

'Everything is useless, how could I take part in such a stupid treasure hunt?' Ragnar shouted then and paced up and down. By now, he had the feeling that his head was about to burst. A dull pain pounded behind his forehead.

'But Ragnar, it was really cool.'

'It was risky. Nothing else.'

'Well, but also interesting.'

'Shut up, you usually mute maggot!'

Annika said nothing anymore, she was shocked.

Ragnar pondered on about himself and bemoaned his fate.

'Why did I set off without a spare wheel?'

Annika was distraught. She was not mute.

'That doesn't actually help, you would have needed four!' was Annika's sarcastic reply.

'Great, wonderful that you're making it worse. Just also turn against me now, go ahead!'

'It's only the truth.'

'The truth is, we shouldn't be here.'

Suddenly, they argued violently. Annika did not know how it could have happened just like that. She got a fright by

Ragnar's behaviour, but she still trusted him deep inside. Had she not yesterday still been his queen?

'It's way too cold. You can freeze to death!' Ragnar added.

'But we have warm blankets.'

'And it's too dangerous for a girl like you, all alone, in the wilderness here.'

'But you're with me.'

'Yes, a stranger. I'm a male stranger.'

'Not anymore.'

'But you, you should be at home,' Ragnar pointed out.

'Why did I take you with me at all? I always cause problems to myself,' Ragnar kept on bemoaning himself.

'Are you really of full age? I'll get into trouble with your parents.'

'Because of last night?'

'Yes, sure. And oh, who knows. In the end, they'll say I kidnapped you!'

Ragnar's face was as red as a lobster. His eyes twinkled. He gasped. His mouth was twisted and open wide.

'We're not allowed to love each other. You're way too young for me.'

'What?' Annika was shocked.

'I don't want to see you ever again!' Ragnar shouted. 'You ruined my life. I hate you!'

He was completely beside himself now. He kept on shouting,

'Oh, I'll have to go now and think. Don't bother me.'

Ragnar stomped off snorting with rage. He kicked firmly at a few small stones that flew away into all directions with a clinking noise. He still felt dizzy, and he experienced a bitter taste in his mouth. His body trembled.

Annika was standing still, she was in shock.

'What's wrong with him? I don't know him like that?'

She cried bitterly. She could not stop sobbing.

'Does he hate me now? How can he be that mean?'

Bit by bit, she gradually began to think logically again. But her brain was working slowly.

'Oh, I need to get help,' she thought in panic. Her heart pounded.

Annika walked along the road. But there was nothing and nobody to be seen.

Annika went a little in the other direction to see if she could get help somehow.

But before she knew it, Ragnar had completely disappeared from her eyeshot. They were separated and she was alone now. She could not find him anymore. Was she lost? What should she do now?

She thought, 'Ragnar, where are you? Please come back. I'm scared!'

There was of course no reply. Ragnar was gone.

She sat down and cried. Thick tears rolled around her cheeks and made her clothing wet. This way, she was freezing even more. She suddenly remembered terrible events at school when she was excluded and left alone as a child. She had to forget the past and calm down. She could only help herself by thoroughly assessing her current situation with all senses.

Suddenly, Annika heard birdsong. She looked up. She saw the sky and a few clouds. A skein of birds passed by over her. Then she looked around; there was Ragnar's car and the road. She felt the air on her skin; she could even feel her toes in the shoe. She was fully present now and not lost in worries about the past or the future.

She smelled smoke. Was there a fire somewhere? But she could not see any smoke. There had to be houses somewhere there that heated their stoves with wood or coal, it was actually cold. She went in the direction Ragnar had taken and where she assumed the origin of the smoke to be. She saw a guesthouse in the distance with a smoking chimney. That probably meant there was a fireplace. Anyway, it looked snug, and she had to seek shelter now. Ragnar was also there, she saw him standing at the reception desk from a distance. He had obviously also seen her and had quickly disappeared. But she was not sure. Could he really be this cold-hearted?

She asked herself why he had not told the lady at the reception desk anything about the broken-down car. The lady was not actually making any attempt to get help. She herself could not tell the female stranger anything; it would have been way too much. She was too scared and too confused to interfere or to think clearly at all. Ragnar had actually just abandoned her, and he had called her a mute maggot. Did he really hate her now? She could not believe it. The tears were unstoppable.

She just managed to get the allegedly last vacant room. She was lucky that the lady offered it to her in an offhanded manner when she was alone with her.

65

The rest of the terrible day went quickly. Annika had bought something to eat from a vending machine. It was not much but it helped with the worst hunger. She could hardly get anything down anyway. She seated herself in the bathtub and allowed the warm water to permeate her skin. She must have sat there for almost an hour. She had forgotten the time completely. But this way, her chilled through body felt better quickly. She had covered herself with lather; the scent of the roses from the shower gel befogged her senses in a pleasant way.

It felt good but her thoughts just circled around in her head. She tried to listen to music to calm herself down, but it did not help. She had to charge her phone and there was a documentary about elephants on TV. When a whodunit came on after that, she turned off the television set. She checked the heating and sat down on her bed. So they both spent the night in this guesthouse in a place on the way from Akureyri to Thingvellir. The accommodation was warm and not too expensive. They both had rooms that were far away from each other, and the mood hit rock bottom for both of them.

Annika felt empty inside. She felt abandoned. She stared at the bare wall. She was still really angry. It came in spates. Thick tears ran over her face that she had burrowed into her pillow.

'How could he do this to me?' she thought and rubbed her eyes. She had loved him. Or not? Meanwhile, her face was red all over and her eyes swollen. Her nose was running, and she looked frantically for handkerchiefs. Information leaflets and a thick telephone book were sitting on the small table below the television set and a box with handkerchiefs was sitting on top of them. Next to them, there was a notepad and a pen. They had really thought of everything here so that the guests could feel comfortable.

Ragnar was glad that he was at the end of the corridor. He did not want to see Annika ever again and certainly did not want to meet her in the hallway. Actually, he told himself that he had already forgotten her. He looked at his mirror image and saw a loser. He had not found the treasure. He threw his golden hat to the ground heedlessly. His teeth were oversized and he saw his students dance in his eyes.

'Ahead, back,' Rita shouted and giggled.

'To the left,' Mona said.

'And to the right,' Karina joined in.

'We're hovering like fairies,' all three of them were singing, out loud. They were wearing bright yellow dresses and had a sunflower in their hair. All girls were draped over and over with jewellery. They were wearing golden necklaces and rings.

Ragnar took off his socks hastily and started dancing barefoot through the room. He laughed hysterically while doing so. Now he was free, and dancing was his life. He felt the warm carpet under the soles of his feet. He then hit the table and a chair toppled over rattling loudly. It did not bother Ragnar. He kept on taking his clothes off.

But the girls' jewellery reminded him of the treasure. He angrily kicked at the waste bin in his room. His foot hurt. His heart also hurt a little, but he hardly felt it. Then he dropped into his bed, tired out. He forgot to switch off the television set, but it turned itself off automatically later.

Annika's room was on the ground floor. This scared her. What if someone came and got in during the night. The probability for that was low. But she was suddenly too tired to think.

66

Shortly before going to bed, Annika was sitting with a hot cup of tea with milk at her desk. She was shaking when she reviewed the terrible events of the day. Her face appeared in the mirror on the wall.

The tea was slowly getting cold.

Annika was suddenly in a breathtaking winter world. Snow was everywhere there. She saw animals that were playing in the snow, and she stopped to watch them. The snow was pure white and crystal clear.

There were polar bears, very cute cubs. They were clumsily sliding down a mountain making happy noises. One of the polar bear cubs bit the other one playfully in the ear. Then it ran away. The other one ran after him and they circled each other like daredevils.

Annika was fascinated by this spectacle. She was not cold despite all the piles of snow and ice. The air smelled of candy floss. She could breathe deeply and kept looking around. Colourful lights were shining above a giant ice rink.

A fully-grown polar bear suddenly appeared. He was also cute. The bear was dancing on the ice, elegantly like a fairy. He was floating over the ice with ease. It was wonderful to watch.

The polar bear was wearing a black top hat and a black suit. His gold tooth flashed up when he smiled.

'Hello, my lovely!' he greeted Annika.

'Where to?'

'Home, please,' she groaned.

'I'm lost.'

'Proceed on your path,' the polar bear said. 'YOU CAN DO THIS!'

A second bear appeared and both bears kissed. This had to be his partner because she was wearing a glistening red dress. Then the bears started dancing. They were spinning round in circles and whirling over the ice like two magicians. Annika had never seen such a beautiful thing. That really had to be fun. Was this the paradise for polar bears?

Then the ice suddenly burst open, and a lively unicorn jumped out. It had a small golden bell around its neck that constantly jingled. A lovely tune. It was wearing a small bow in the colours of the rainbow around his horn. The unicorn was joyfully dancing and singing. Annika found the scene very beautiful. The polar bears laughed and clapped enthusiastically.

But the hole in the ice got bigger. It started to consume the entire area. Annika could not keep her balance anymore and she got pulled into the deep water. The ice-cold water made her freeze immediately. She fell into a bottomless abyss.

'YOU CAN DO THIS!' was the echo she heard in her mind.

She was floating.

Was she dead? She should be panicking but she felt strangely calm. Could you be both completely excited and very calm at the same time?

'Is dying that easy?' the thought crossed her mind.

'YOU CAN DO THIS!' she heard the polar bear shout again.

'Am I out of control, what is this?' she thought hectically.

She kept on falling.

Fell and fell.

'YOU CAN DO THIS!' both of the polar bears and the unicorn chanted in unison now.

'Help!' she finally shouted loudly.

But nobody could hear her. She was stuck in the water.

Like under a blanket, trapped with no chance of rescue.

'YOU CAN DO THIS!'

Then she suddenly heard a muffled ringing of a different kind, an alarm clock. She opened her eyes and took a deep breath.

She was lying in her bed in her room. Her clothes wringing with sweat.

Everything had just been a dream.

67

Annika did not usually dream a lot. At least, she could not particularly remember many dreams. But since she had set the alarm clock, it could happen sometimes that she woke up in the middle of a dream. But this dream seemed important to her. It came surprisingly and was still so useful. Now, where she felt so terrible, perhaps it brought help.

'YOU CAN DO THIS!' she thought. 'Yes, ... yes, of course!'

She had to write this down immediately. Otherwise, she would forget her dream very quickly. After all, the dream was also about dancing. Was that a sign that she had a future with Ragnar? And there was something else.

The dream had made Annika realise that she had to try and proceed on her path. She could do it. But how? What was the right path? It was still very early in the morning. Annika brooded over it intensely. She resolved to act. She had to try despite of all her anxiety. But what could she do to sort things out with Ragnar? Could she do something to make his car roadworthy again?

Annika furrowed her brows.

New hope emerged in her.

She had to come up with something quickly.

68

Annika had to get help if they still wanted to continue with the treasure hunt. Perhaps there was still a chance and Ragnar had come to his senses? She ventured out. But there was nobody at the reception desk this early.

'If only I knew which room Ragnar is in,' she thought with a heavy heart. 'I hope he's well.'

She could not wake up all the people in their rooms that early. That is why she sneaked back to her room on tiptoe. The corridor appeared to be endlessly long to her. Briefly, she believed that she would never find her room again. There was only this panic that showed its ugly head time after time. But Annika was stronger now. She breathed deeply in and out.

'YOU CAN DO THIS!' echoed in Annika's thoughts.

That gave her courage to push forward. Slowly but unerringly she reached her room and sat down on a chair. She stared at the ceiling.

'What shall I do?' she thought.

Suddenly, she had an idea.

She had to call the breakdown service or find a repair shop nearby. Her phone had been charged overnight and she also remembered the telephone book on the table. This way she would certainly find a local shop without needing to search for long. She could also search online if need be if she had a good broadband connection. She had not checked that yet.

'YOU CAN DO THIS!'

There was that thought again. It was in her mind and really pushed her on now. It was like a fire inside her. There was no going back. Hiding and doing nothing was yesterday. Today, Annika had to work up the courage.

Annika just had to find help no matter how big the anxiety was. She had never called any strangers before, but it had to be now. Her mother had usually helped her, but nobody was here now to rescue her out of her necessity. Not even Ragnar.

She flicked through the telephone book. There was a part where everything was sorted by trades. She found a list of car repair shops. Not many but she had to try them in turn. She wanted to dial the number of the first shop in the telephone book, but she hesitated before making the call.

Eventually, she took pen and paper. These were also still on the table in her room. She wrote down how the conversation could go. What did she have to say? There was her name, what happened and where she was. No, where the car was. A few bullet points had to be enough. She just needed these to manage the conversation successfully. Prepared like that, she hoped that it would be fine.

She put the slip with the notes in front of herself and went through the conversation again in her mind. At the smallest trace of thoughts of giving up, the dream crossed her mind again.

'YOU CAN DO THIS!'

She was strongly determined to do it. Now or never!

She eventually typed the number on her phone. Her hands trembled so much that she entered a wrong digit and had to start again. Then the number was correct. She checked the number several times because she did not want to bother the wrong person and then say nothing. To have to apologise for dialling the wrong number would be more difficult than everything else.

She finally pressed the symbol on the phone to dial the number. The dial tone made her even more uneasy. But she would make it, nobody was listening now. She was alone in this room.

'Good morning. Car repair shop Bon Voyage here. Who am I speaking with?'

Annika hesitated.

'Hello?'

'Yes. ... Annika Magnusdottir. ... We have four flat tyres.'

Annika breathed. It went quite well.

'The car is sitting here... Yes, thank you!'

The conversation went well. At least, the member of staff off of the repair shop would say that afterwards but for Annika the experience was very different. She felt terribly nervous and believed to not have uttered any reasonable words. But she had explained the problem to the man, and she could be helped. The company wanted to pick up the car immediately and Annika was supposed to go to it and wait for the breakdown lorry.

It was still a little dark outside. Annika went along the road and looked for the car. Where was it? She heard birds chirp in the distance. A sign that it was getting light soon. The cold air made her alert.

She eventually saw the car. It was sitting there, just as lonely as yesterday. The golden colour was eye-catching compared to the grey road. She saw the entire extent of the destruction, four tyres without any air. She remembered that she had no car keys. Ragnar had run away angrily, had he locked the car at all? She checked the door handle. The car doors were open, and the ignition key was still in the lock.

'Oh, we're lucky, nobody's stolen it,' Annika thought gladly. 'How careless, don't do that again, Ragnar.'

Ragnar had just disappeared yesterday but she herself had also not thought of locking up because of all the stress. The luggage was also still there, too.

'That's really only possible here,' she thought. Then she saw a bag of cat food.

Suddenly, she thought of Felix. Where was the cat?

She had not noticed until now that Felix was not there. She felt panic. Just then she heard a quiet meowing. Blankets were in the back seat. Felix crept out of his hiding place under the seat. He had probably hidden there all night long. Annika took him into her arms and stroked him.

The breakdown lorry from the garage not far away finally came and loaded up Ragnar's car. Annika was supposed to go with them in the driver's cab. She hesitated but she knew she had to go to find out where they were taking the car and if they could fix it quickly. After all, it was not every day that four tyres needed to be replaced.

She got in and sat down next to the driver in the passenger seat. Felix was allowed to accompany her. He was very quiet.

The view from the lorry was different, you felt like a giant, as you were sitting higher up than in a regular car. Annika knew the feeling very well because her father was also a truck driver. In the past, as a child, she had often got in his truck and pretended she was driving. She had liked it a lot to hold the big wheel and to touch the shift lever. Sometimes, he had also taken her for a trip because she loved cruising around in the world. It felt like freedom.

She buckled her seatbelt and waited curiously. Would the driver want to talk with her? Her anxiety proved unfounded because he hardly said anything during the journey. But it only took a few minutes.

The repair shop in this area was prepared for everything, especially tyre problems. They had fitting tyres in the right size available. They would have it sorted out and ready in no time. Annika left the payment to Ragnar when he came to pick up the car. He would surely not mind that she had taken care of everything else.

It did not matter now, as Annika had to go back to her accommodation. She had to talk to Ragnar urgently and convince him to continue with the treasure hunt.

In view of what she had just achieved, all by herself, they just had to continue the journey. Otherwise, all of it would have been for nothing. She could walk back to the guesthouse or see whether there was a bus. She would not give up that easily. Actually she had never given up in her life but certainly not now.

'YOU CAN DO THIS!'

A bird passed her from above. She watched it fly.

'Exactly. Forward and not back.'

69

When Ragnar woke up, he was shocked. Where was he? He could not remember anything. The room was untidy, and it seemed strange to him.

'When did I arrive here?' he thought. 'Did I have a nightmare?'

Fragments came back to his mind. 'Where was Annika? And what was going on with the treasure?'

'I was on the move with her,' he thought. 'Annika.'

He got hot. He still did not feel fully fit.

'We were looking for a treasure.'

He put his feet to the ground and wanted to get up. But he had to sit down again, as he got dizzy immediately.

'What's wrong with me?' he thought, bewildered. 'Am I ill?'

He tried again. This time very slowly. He carefully felt his way into the bathroom and looked at himself in the mirror. He was unshaved and somehow pale. The guesthouse had kindly provided towels, soap and shampoo for free. There was also a disposable razor.

After using the bathroom Ragnar noticed that his luggage was not there. He put his clothes from yesterday on and went outside. It was already light and the air made him alert. He breathed in deeply. Every breath felt refreshing.

Where was his car?

His memories of yesterday slowly came back. They made him panic. Was it not damaged? All tyres were flat.

He looked around. Nobody was at the reception desk. There was also nobody to be seen outside. He went along the road. But Ragnar could not find his car anywhere, so he went back to the house.

Annika arrived back at the accommodation again. Felix was with her. She was just looking for her room key when she suddenly stopped short. There was Ragnar! She recognised him clearly by his golden hat. He had also recognised her, and he was waving. She quickly ran towards him.

'Annika, I'm so glad to see you! What's going on here? Where's my car?' he exclaimed.

'Didn't we have four flat tyres?'

'All done,' she replied abruptly. 'The car is in the repair shop and you can pick it up soon.'

'Did you take care of the car?'

'Yes, I did.'

'Thank you, Annika. That's great. And you did that all by yourself!' Ragnar beamed.

'I'm so proud of you.'

Annika blushed. She could certainly do more than people would credit her. Did she have to get praised for that specifically? But it felt good to experience Ragnar as a nice person again.

'I've only organised the repair so that we can go on. We'll be driving on, will we? You didn't want to ever see me again yesterday!'

'Not want to ever see you again? What are you talking about?'

'You were really angry. That's what you said. So... How are you today?'

But Ragnar did not know for sure what he was feeling.

'I believe I wasn't myself yesterday. No idea. Somehow I feel sick, as if I'd celebrated a mega party yesterday. And this headache...'

'I think you're ill.'

'Oh, no party then? And why do I not know anything anymore? I need to go to a doctor's immediately.'

Ragnar was bewildered but he did not want to lose Annika. Could he possibly have a brain tumour? It did not matter at this moment.

'Annika please, I'm so sorry. Let's forget this nonsense. I didn't want to hurt you if I have. I'm really very sorry. You're my queen. I love you!'

Annika looked on expressionless.

'Annika, I love you,' Ragnar repeated desperately. 'Really. I do love you.'

This emotional rollercoaster was unbearable. And Annika knew exactly what she felt deep inside her heart.

'I'll forgive you. I'm sorry, too,' Annika declared.

'I love you, too.'

Ragnar was relieved.

Annika and Ragnar gazed at each other, understanding each other without words. They kissed swiftly. Then another more lingering kiss followed. They had both closed their eyes.

This song about paradise crossed Ragnar's mind. He was suddenly dancing. His legs were rhythmically moving to imaginary music, back and forth.

'Love really sends you to paradise,' he thought and his entire body tingled as if his extremities had pins and needles. He felt as if he heard wedding bells toll in his mind.

'This is the best day of my life.'

Annika smiled after the kiss.

'I'll always be there for you,' Ragnar said and smiled back. 'From now on, really. I promise!'

70

Ragnar was feeling much better. He could concentrate without problems again and his headache was also gone. He did not think about his mysterious illness anymore.

After the car had been repaired and fitted with a complete set of new tyres, Ragnar and Annika visited the place of the last clue, Thingvellir. There were no problems during the journey and at the destination a few free car park spaces were available. They stopped, got out and wandered around aimlessly. Their eyes fell on a big electronic display board illuminating the place. The screen was giant, and it showed non-stop advertising for various Icelandic sights. Colourful pictures showed the most beautiful waterfalls from all sides.

'Very modern here,' Ragnar said and did not pay it much attention.

'Yes, it's actually a World Heritage Site,' Annika had read this and added, 'I think the only one in the whole of Iceland!'

'Well, that's really very impressive.'

There was also a church nearby and lots of water. It was actually a huge plain with a rift with high rocks to the left and right with a few mountains in the background. They were bare. There was a narrow footpath that went along between the rocks. Not all parts of the mountain range would be accessible depending on the weather conditions.

'Is this the famous Law Rock?' Ragnar asked and pointed to a particularly prominent summit in the distance.

'I don't know where exactly it is. But the laws used to be declared there.' Annika knew a lot about Iceland's history. She felt the cold wind on her legs.

'Sure, that's quite clear to me. It's already in the name.'

They laughed. Felix was in Annika's arms. He meowed loudly. They were just standing there and looked around. The view was breathtaking.

Suddenly, Anton joined them. He had been waiting for them. He had at least hoped that they would come, as he could not find any further clues to the whereabouts of the treasure on his own here.

His guilty conscience had been troubling him. Hopefully, nothing had happened to Ragnar. Surely, they had found help and got new tyres. Even though that would probably have been expensive. The thought of money made him anxious because he remembered his debts with startling clarity.

Just for fun, the chewing gum he had given Ragnar had contained a mood changing substance. The pressure on him was unbearable. Recently, more and more often he was tortured by thoughts that he was a bad person.

But when Ragnar and Annika saw him, he was the big strong Anton again. With his head held high, he went towards them.

'So that you know, that was me!' he boasted proudly and clenched his fist as if he wanted to start a fight.

Ragnar raised his hand defensively in front of his face and backed off instinctively. Anton let them know that he had intentionally crashed into their car, stolen their provisions and punctured their tyres.

'And besides, there was something in the chewing gum that has heated you up properly, hasn't it? And I have just followed you; I haven't really found or solved the clues myself. Except for the one in Akureyri where I was really lucky!' Anton admitted.

Annika was pale. Of course, they had already suspected that he might be behind all that. Ragnar confronted him. His golden hat made him appear taller than he was in reality, and it seemed to give him an air of authority.

'Listen. Destroying things, stealing, hurting others, that gets you nowhere. What would your mother say to that?'

Anton paused for a moment.

'My mother?'

'She'd surely be deeply ashamed for what you have done. You discredited her. Her and your entire family. Every mother wants a decent son.'

'What?' He yelled.

'Come on, calm down. Breathe deeply. Come on.'

Anton did what he had been told. He became calmer. He thought of his mother and suddenly he saw how much she must have been suffering. And he realised that he was suffering. He noticed his guilt deep inside. He felt literally he was being crushed to death by it like by heavy stones being placed on his chest. He was unusually quiet and lowered his gaze, as if there was a treasure buried in the ground.

Ragnar kept on talking.

'Keep on breathing. Everything's going to be alright.'

Anton was pensive. He trembled visibly.

He regretted what he had done. He spoke softly.

'I was stupid.'

There was a pause. His voice stalled, as he was fighting back his tears.

'I'm so sorry.'

'It's alright,' Ragnar said. 'We'll forgive you.'

'I'm afraid there's no forgiveness,' Anton lamented.

'There is,' Ragnar said. 'There's something good in every human.'

Annika nodded tentatively. Anton rubbed his eyes and he shed a tear. Soon it was an entire ocean full of tears.

He would have been ashamed of crying in public in the past. He had not done this in his entire life. He was not allowed to. But now he had realised that he could show his emotions openly even as a man. It helped him to regulate his inner world.

After a long silence, Anton spoke.

'I don't deserve a treasure. I cheated.'

'True.'

'Of course, I would like to pay for the damage to your car and the tyres.'

'Well, we'll manage that.'

'Unfortunately, I don't have any money, that's why I really wanted to find the treasure in the first place. I'm up to my neck in debt.'

'Oh, we're so sorry,' Ragnar said and looked to Annika. 'But you'll find help if you look for it. For your finances and for your anger.'

Anton nodded, hardly visible. He thought of his mother who had never looked for and never found help. And he thought of his father who had had the same experience. He would do better.

'We'll get that sorted out, Anton,' Ragnar reassured him.

'Thanks,' Anton said. 'You're the best.'

Then Gunnar and Colette joined them. She was officially his new girlfriend now. Gunnar finally believed that he was over the pain of losing his first wife. They had ensconced themselves in Akureyri for a while but had finally also found the clue at the fish factory.

'What's going on here?' Gunnar asked, bewildered, and he looked at Ragnar.

'We've made peace.'

Ragnar explained briefly what had happened. Gunnar nodded.

'Oh, I see.'

Suddenly, it was very quiet.

They all hugged each other.

71

They were all still standing there when they realised that the treasure had still not been found. Was there another clue here?

'Where can it be?' Ragnar puzzled as he was examining the grass.

Felix was sniffing on a branch and started flexing his claws. Then he began digging a hole in the soil with his paws.

'Is the treasure there?' Ragnar wondered and went to him. He could not see anything in the hole except dug-over soil and an earthworm. Felix showed no interest in the worm and eventually ran away.

'Hardly,' Ragnar thought and went back to the others.

'Now we're actually here,' Ragnar said thoughtfully and fiddled with his jacket.

'Here, the national parliament used to meet. Now it's a national park.'

He had learnt more about the Silfra rift that was nearby at the tourist information. It runs under water and the ground ruptures there, as the American plate and the Eurasian plate drift apart.

'That's on the same rupture line as the bridge between the continents that we visited at the start of the treasure hunt on the Reykjanes peninsula. But in the Silfra rift, you cannot walk along but dive.'

Anton had heard everything.

'How interesting,' he thought.

Ragnar was now searching the meadow on the other side. His golden hat hid the sweat on his forehead. But he was not going to give up.

Anton felt slightly better now, and Annika was standing next to him. Apparently, he now had his feelings under control.

'I'm really sorry about that stupid chat-up line,' Anton said softly. 'I'm just like that. I didn't mean to scare you.'

She said nothing but he kept on talking.

'I hope that's forgotten?'

She nodded.

'Look,' Gunnar suddenly shouted from afar. They all ran towards him.

'Colette discovered this!'

With their eyes wide open, they were all looking at the giant advertising display in the car park now.

There was the entire poem with all its stanzas clearly visible for all:

In this corner starts great fortune
Examine the connection, do it soon
Where Europe and America meet
Your dreams came true greet!

Further into the mainland, go
Where Strokkur provides a show
Come to the Great Geysir
The path to joy is here!

Where the water flows
Vigorously down it goes
Look behind, walk under
Get chipper watching a wonder!

There is a mountain up close
Its giant size really shows
A dragon lives inside
Fire and ash are in its might!

Where the ground is so black
Look for the lava in a stack
Endless expanses of sand to reach
You might find things on the beach!

The glacier becomes a lake
Progress you make
Drivin' or swimmin'
You need to determine!

By the fjords in the East
No ferry costs, at least
Just look at the port
And success will not fall short!

Further northbound like the wind
You really must obey this hint
A waterfall is coming along
Dettifoss is big and strong!

Go, it's much at stake
To a volcanic mosquito lake
Mineral-rich water is healthy
This place makes you wealthy!

Now visit a lovely town
Famous for its fish industry and a crown
Take the westbound road even in snow and ice
Then, you will find your great prize!

Come to the ancient parliament valley
The best location for a rally
Geologically active, beautiful scenery
A national park, as it should be!

And a new stanza:
Iceland is beautiful, my dear
You realize this right here
You saw and learnt a lot
You just hit the jackpot!

72

Inga emerged and smiled.

'Oh, you've already discovered it,' she exclaimed happily.

'Such a lovely poem!'

'Yes,' someone said.

'I like the rhymes.'

'Poetry! Something new!' a visitor was amazed. 'Look!'

'Ha-ha.'

'Although there's no treasure in terms of massive wealth here, the treasure hunt still had a meaning.'

Inga pointed to the text. In her floaty coat, she looked like a mighty eagle that watched over everything. She was exceptionally suited to this role.

'You are all winners!' she added happily and spread her arms wide.

'We can all learn from this.'

The others agreed. They were completely overwhelmed by the surprising change of the events.

'I hope the treasure hunt was fun. I, for one, really enjoyed it.'

Inga revealed that she had organised everything this way.

'Fridrik Jonsson was my grandfather. He had a preference for the extravagant. He convinced me before his death to play this game with a few randomly chosen people. With you.' Inga briefly paused, then she continued calmly.

'After all, the old Fridrik was a man with brains. He wanted all the participants to get to know the country, this country, better. The protection of nature was very important to him. That is why he also has donated a large amount of his assets to a charity that will ensure that the beauty of Iceland will be conserved forever.'

Inga had taken care of all the clues and made sure that they were in the right place at the right time, and she had also monitored who was where on the route at any given time.

'Then the plane at the waterfall was sent by you?' Ragnar asked with interest and smiled at her nicely.

'Yes,' her answer was concise. However, after a short pause, she realised that she had to explain it.

'I sent it when I knew all those still taking part were at the waterfall.'

'And the message on the radio?' Gunnar exclaimed in disbelief.

'Yes, that, too. I arranged for that, yes,' Inga replied. 'When it was time for the next clue.'

'And the message in the bottle, too? And the sign on the fence and the flag?'

'Yes, precisely all clues.'

'Ingenious, I'm flabbergasted,' Ragnar retorted.

'Me too,' Gunnar said. 'Rather!'

Anton agreed. Annika also nodded gently.

Inga laughed. The corners of her mouth were moving up and down gently while she continued talking.

'And now this. It's the right place for this lovely poem, isn't it?'

Again, everybody agreed.

'I will make sure that the participants who dropped out of the race early get to hear what the whole purpose of this treasure hunt was. Granny Helga, Jonas, Sigrun, Margret and Oskar would certainly like to know,' Inga continued to explain.

'We can all learn from this.'

'Perhaps someone else would like to hang the poem on the wall,' somebody joked.

'Not a bad idea,' Ragnar said. 'I'll think about that. Or what do you think, Annika?'

She nodded.

It was not difficult to take a photo of the big display board with the poem on it. This time, Annika's phone was fully charged. Her mother would be amazed about what her daughter had experienced.

Anton was disappointed that there was no treasure at all. No gold, no money - for anybody. He apologised to Inga for his bad behaviour, and she had shown understanding. He really needed help to sort out his life again, he had grasped this fully now. It was not too late yet. And he also badly wanted to dive in this Silfra rift!

Gunnar and Colette were too much in love to be sad about the non-existing treasure. They had decided to go on holiday to France together. Completely without a treasure hunt but with good food and lots of exercise. She wanted to introduce him to her family and show him another country. Now that they knew Iceland well, it was time for the rest of the world. Perhaps they would marry in Paris.

Inga recounted that she often used to be out and about with her grandfather.

'He has shown me things that hardly anyone knows. He was very wise.'

Inga had noticed that Annika hardly spoke. She said that she herself as a child was also this quiet. She must have had a fear of communication in the past. She had recognised this one day. But now, she was changing the world of science with her long-standing research on selective mutism and social anxiety disorders.

'It would be wonderful if people recognised such difficulties in young children in the future, so they were able to get appropriate help quickly. Then nobody would need to grow to adulthood with this anymore.'

Annika nodded in agreement.

73

After all participants had digested the adventurous events of this treasure hunt and especially the poetic end at Thingvellir, life went on as normal. The surprising result had actually been that there had not been any treasure in the shape of gold and money at all but only the insight to know and love Iceland better.

Annika's life with her selective mutism was still full of challenges that other people could not imagine. There were big and small obstacles in daily life all the time, where she actually needed to talk and still sometimes thought,

'NO ONE MUST HEAR!'

But she was not alone with her problems any longer. There were people who knew. Ragnar wanted to help her as much as he could. Professor Inga Hansdottir was also ready to offer her guidance and advice.

With the help of the dream about the polar bears, Annika had realised that it helped to face her fears and to try new things. The thought of

'YOU CAN DO THIS!' would now be in her mind often and it would push her on further.

She collected information about available therapies for adults and had made friends with others suffering with similar issues online in social networks. That helped her to understand everything better and to find her true self. Peer support was really very helpful.

Since she had started therapy with an experienced female speech and language therapist who knew a lot about selective mutism, she was already talking a little more. She needed a relaxed atmosphere and no pressure to speak. People had to give her space to develop without fear of punishment. She should be able to feel safe. That way, she could tolerate others hearing her voice. And she had to tackle her anxiety of certain situations in small steps by starting with easy tasks and slowly working towards a bigger goal. It was still difficult for her to contribute to groups with many strangers. But she had gained more self-confidence through this treasure hunt. Soon, she would surely be able to give her opinions more often.

She had also undergone behavioural therapy with a psychologist where she learnt how to reinterpret her thoughts. She should not view everything so negatively. Healthy optimism was good. The glass was half full in the future, not half empty. And she learnt that she did not need to worry about all the things in the world that she could not influence as an individual herself. Instead, from now on Annika was grateful for the things that she was able to control and experience every day. For example, for her participation in the treasure hunt.

Furthermore, she had obtained relaxation music and was considering hypnosis. That way, she could influence her subconscious emotions directly; anyway this is what she had read. She had also learnt to like herself the way she was.

She had really read a lot and was almost a little overwhelmed by the diversity of therapy options. And if all these would not help, medication together with therapy was also an alternative.

She was also interested in horse riding lessons as she had heard that an animal could potentially also help with anxiety issues. And she had wanted to learn how to ride a horse since she had seen the horses at the lake. But she could not try everything at the same time. She also needed help with her fear of dogs. And she already had Felix who gave her a lot of pleasure.

Felix the cat stayed with Annika. He had to go to the vet soon to make sure that he really was not injured and to receive any necessary examinations and treatments. But he had become Annika's best fluffy friend. And he also allowed her to transport him in his cage without much ado now.

Max the teddy was still there to watch over Annika's sleep. Most of the time, he was just sitting there because she rarely played with him. But he made Annika feel safe and was there to get cuddled when necessary.

Ragnar wanted to support Annika in all she did. His job was still fun. Perhaps she could dance with him? Surely she could learn it. He was sure that it would help her to relax. And she could express herself non-verbally with her body through movement and without needing to speak.

Once Ragnar took Annika along to his dancing school and she watched happily. His golden hat sat securely on his head when he was dancing. Forward, back, side, together. He sometimes came up with new dancing steps, especially when he was happy.

His staff members had taken good care of his dance studio during his absence. His students Mona, Rita and Karina had even invented a new fairy dance that attracted young customers. Somehow Ragnar had strange fragments of memory; he saw all three of them dressed as fairies in bright yellow dresses and with sunflowers in their hair gliding across the dance floor. He would dance along as their sorcerer now that he was back again. The new course promised to be a bestseller.

Annika and Ragnar were in love. Indeed, they were not yet planning a wedding, but it could not be ruled out in the future. Annika primarily wanted to spend time on her education and even though she perhaps wanted her own children later, for a start, she would concentrate on studying.

Since taking part in the treasure hunt, she was very interested in the history of the Icelandic geography. She had started attending university and she also received official support for her selective mutism there. For example, at first she was allowed to record talks at home and to play the video at the seminar. Later on, she was able to give speeches in front of a smaller group of students. Annika made a few friends at university with whom she often studied. She knew so much and sometimes she could explain things for them that they had not understood during the lectures.

Annika had also decided to become more independent. In the long run, she planned to move out from her parents and earn her own money. And she wanted to learn how to drive to be better able to reach remote places.

She also wanted to do more with Ragnar in her spare time. Both hoped to be able to enjoy every moment together. Just in the here and now without dwelling on the past or fearing the future.

One day both of them went for a walk in the garden.

'I'd like to go hiking with you. Just you and me.'

'Let's explore the highlands in the heart of the country.'

'That's a great idea. Count me in.'

Ragnar and Annika had a new task.

Annika had achieved personal growth during this exciting time of the treasure hunt and was ready for all the challenges that life would throw at her now.

'YOU CAN DO THIS!' Annika thought and she smiled contently in Ragnar's arms.

74

It is possible that the whole treasure hunt was just an invented story that Annika Magnusdottir had made up.

In case she would like to become a writer in the future, she would certainly be very talented. Writing is one of her greatest strengths. As well as creativity. These are quiet strengths.

That is why, as the attentive reader might possibly already have spotted, perhaps some things might not have corresponded quite well to reality because, as it is well known, there are no limits to a young person's imagination.

Acknowledgements

I am very grateful to everyone who supported me with the creation of this book. I am indebted to my publisher and editor Mandy Collins for her invaluable assistance. Thanks also to Kathy Rowan for her cover art and map and also to Mark Hetherington for cover design. Special thanks go to Wilma Burnett, Christine Winter and Dr Siebke Melfsen for reading the manuscript and providing helpful feedback. I also would like to thank my family and friends for their patience.

Author Biography

Dr Antje Bothin has a passion for creative work. She particularly loves travelling and takes great pleasure in writing about nature, the human mind and the world around her. She grew up in Germany and has lived experience of Selective Mutism. She has an academic background with a first degree in Business Engineering and an MSc in Information and Media Technology and successfully completed a PhD in Information Studies at the University of Sheffield. She also works as a translator and tutor. She has authored scientific papers, short stories and poems. Her poetry has been published in international anthologies. This is her first novel. She enjoys living in Scotland and when not writing, reading or drinking tea, she can be found cycling in the countryside or volunteering for local charities.

Printed in Great Britain
by Amazon

37722839R00108